To Lila,

Thanks for reading
Secret in the Sand.

Love,
Margy

August 2017

Secret in the Sand

Margaret Turner Taylor

ISBN: 978-1-54391-010-0

Cover design by Jaime L. Coston
Author photo by Andrea López Burns
Interior design and layout by Jamie Tipton, Open Heart Designs

This book is dedicated with all my love to
Lane Taylor Worthing

Contents

– Chapter One –
On the Beach.. 1

– Chapter Two –
By the Sea.. 9

– Chapter Three –
By the Beautiful Sea................................. 17

– Chapter Four –
The Winds of War 31

– Chapter Five –
The Second Happy Time 41

– Chapter Six –
Reinhard's Gold 47

– Chapter Seven –
Smile! 59

– Chapter Eight –
The Wise Man Arrives.............................. 70

– Chapter Nine –
Old Money 79

– Chapter Ten –
The Summer of '42 86

– Chapter Eleven –
I've Got Plenty of Nothin' 96

– Chapter Twelve –
Time Changes Everything 108

– Chapter Thirteen –
I Have a Photograph 115

– Chapter Fourteen –
I Have a Photograph, Too 120

– Chapter Fifteen –
Pieces of the Puzzle 124

– Chapter Sixteen –
Back to the Future 129

Preface

I proposed writing a book for my granddaughter, Lane, and asked her what kind of book she would like for it to be. She said she would like a book about "magic." I told her I thought I could write a book about buried treasure. She said that would be good, too.

When I submitted the book for Lane's approval, she liked the story and picked up a number of typos I had missed. Sharp eyes! She wanted the book to be longer and requested more thorough development of a couple of the characters. She wanted a more definite resolution of some loose ends. She pointed out an inconsistency or two in the story line and was a superb editor and critic. I took all of her suggestions into account in my corrections and revisions.

Lane is not yet a teenager. So many books written for Lane's reading level are about teenage angst, boyfriends, romance, and all of that stuff. When she gets to that point in her life, she will have plenty of books to read. My goal with Lane's book was to write a story with an interesting and exciting plot and a challenging vocabulary, without the usual teenager story lines.

I wanted Lane to learn something about a period of history that has been important in my own life. I wanted to bring alive for her, in a thought-provoking and stimulating way, the period of World War II, and I wanted to motivate her to read more history. I hope that Lane, her cousins, and others her age will want to learn more about the past, its successes and its failures. I hope that after reading *Secret in the Sand*, the younger generation will want to study history and to learn from it. As George Santayana said, "Those who cannot remember the past are condemned to repeat it."

Acknowledgments

My granddaughter Lane was my guide and critic before, during, and after I wrote Secret in the Sand. This book was written for her. She chose the title, and her suggestions along the way made this a much better story.

Special thanks to Jane, Peggy, and Kristen for reading and telling me what resonated and what needed to be changed or omitted. Many thanks to other readers: Margaret, Amy, Josie, Angus, Meredith, Turner, Teddy, Louisa, Richard, and Katherine.

My husband Robert and his cousin, John Corley, author of A House Divided, both contributed careful readings, edits, and commentary on technical points and the story as a whole. Thanks, Corley boys. John's military expertise was particularly helpful in my efforts to get the U-boat part of the story right.

The first question Elizabeth Burke, M.D. always asked me when I saw her in her office was: "What's new and exciting in your life?" I promised myself that one day I would have a good answer for her. Thank you, Dr. Burke.

Thanks to my excellent and patient editor and publicist Lynn Wiese Sneyd who is teaching me the craft and the art. She has been tireless in her efforts to turn this academic writer into a storyteller. Thanks, Lynn! No more dull!

– Chapter One –

On the Beach

Last Summer

Lane and Louisa were digging to China. The two cousins had been working all morning with their shovels and pails and had made an enormous hole in the sand. They could both get into the hole at the same time, and they were hoping the incoming tide did not wipe away their great accomplishment. It was almost lunchtime. They knew they would have to abandon their marvelous chasm when their mothers told them they had to leave the beach and get out of the sun. Louisa scooped another bucket of sand out of the hole and reached for a shiny object that peeked through the surface. The girls had found sand crabs, pieces of glass, shells, a few beer can tabs, and a plastic whistle in their big dig, but they had not found any money—much to their chagrin.

"I think I have money," Louisa shouted.

"No, you don't," Lane told her. Lane had just turned eleven and was the older and more knowledgeable cousin. "You thought those beer can things were money, and they turned out to be junk. There's no money here. Those people with metal detectors come out early in the morning and get all the money and valuable stuff off the beach. My dad told me so."

"No, it really is money. Look." Louisa, who was seven, handed the gold coin to Lane who carefully examined it.

"It's not real money. It's just pretend money. It looks like one of those tokens you get at the Jolly Roger or on the Rehoboth Boardwalk. I know my money, and it isn't a penny or a nickel or a dime or a quarter. And that's all the round money there is. It's not even the right color, but it is a nice gold color. It's heavy, too. Heavier than real money. It has a king's face on it. We don't have kings any more in the United States." Lane took real money to buy her lunch at school so she was sure the coin she held in her hand was not the real thing. She also knew about dollars and how to make change. What more was there to know?

Lane's mother was standing at the top of the wooden stairs that crossed the dune and led down to the beach. She waved at the two tow-headed girls and shouted that it was time for them to come up to the house. Lane put the coin in the pocket of her shorts. "Don't tell your mom or my mom what we found, okay?"

"Okay, but I found it so you don't get to keep it."

The girls ran across the sand to where Lane's mother, Gretchen, was waiting for them. "Did you get to China?" she asked the girls. "That hole looks pretty big to me."

Lane mumbled, "Not yet." She didn't want to reveal anything about what they'd found.

They raced ahead of Gretchen to the big gray-shingled beach house. The sooner they ate their lunch and the sooner they started their hour-long mandatory after-lunch rest period, the sooner they could get back to digging and either finding China or finding treasure. The wooden screen door banged behind them as they ran into the house and took their

seats at the table. Their brothers were already eating sandwiches and demolishing a veggie tray with ranch dressing.

"I have turkey on whole wheat, tuna salad on wheat,
and tomato and cheese on white. I also have wonderful
watermelon for dessert." Louisa and Tyler's mother, Abbey,
was taking orders for lunch. "If you eat your sandwich, you
can have a second handful of chips. Pickles are free, and
lemonade is free."

Lane took the coin from her pocket and flashed it ever so
briefly at Louisa. She didn't think either Tyler or Robbie saw
it before she put it away.

"What was that you just put in your pocket?" Tyler
wanted to know. He was nine and noticed everything. No
one ever got away with anything around Tyler.

"Nothing, really. We were digging to China and found
some stuff in the sand." Lane tried to be casual and non-com-
mittal.

Robbie chimed in. "You can't really dig to China, you
know. No matter how deep you dig, you will never get to
China." Robbie was the youngest of the four cousins, but
he was a stickler for the facts and a very literal judge of all
conversations. "You have to go through the earth's core to
get to China, and there is molten metal in the earth's core. It's
so hot it will kill you in a minute. Also, the earth is almost
eight thousand miles in diameter. Nobody can dig that far,
not even the President."

Lane told her six-year-old brother he took the fun out of
everything, but she was glad to have the discussion changed
from the coin in her pocket.

"You'll never find any money or jewels in the sand, you
know. The people with the metal detectors get out to the beach
as soon as the sun comes up, and they find all the good stuff."
Robbie had heard the same comments from his dad about the
futility of finding anything valuable by digging at the beach.

Tyler took another handful of chips. "I found a grad-
uation ring from Ohio State, class of 1954, with a big red
ruby in it. That was valuable." He had found the ring three
years earlier.

"Not really very valuable," Louisa retorted. "Nobody
wanted it, and you still have it. What are you going to do with
it? How many arcade games can you play with the money
you made from finding that ring?" She was skeptical about
her brother's accomplishments.

"Okay, everybody clean their plates and take them over
to the sink," Gretchen announced. " Time for a rest or a nap
or whatever you want to do that is quiet for the next hour."
Gretchen enforced the quiet hour because she wanted the kids
to wind down and read, and she wanted to keep them out of
the sun during the hottest part of the day. "I'll take everyone
who is very quiet during rest hour down to Bethany for ice
cream. If you're rowdy, you don't get ice cream." Having
four kids in the same room was not conducive to keeping the
rowdy factor low. Bribes were essential.

Lane and Louisa looked at each other and sighed. They
had hoped to return immediately to digging in the sand and
maybe finding more gold money. Ice cream was a good thing,
however, and not to be dismissed lightly. After they'd had
ice cream, they'd resume their project. For the next hour,
all four kids observed quiet hour in the bunk room of their
grandparents' beach house in Sandpiper Dunes.

When Lane and Louisa returned to the beach later that
afternoon, the incoming tide had not yet reached their hole.
Both girls climbed into the excavation and began to dig again.
They looked at each other in surprise when their plastic
shovels hit something hard. They dropped their shovels and
excitedly began scraping the sand away with their hands.
Neither Lane nor Louisa could believe it when they uncovered
a large and very rusty metal box. It was so heavy they couldn't

lift it or budge it an inch. They were naturally curious but at the same time reluctant to touch something that looked like it might be dangerous. Maybe this was grown-up stuff? Maybe it would explode? Maybe they needed to ask their parents about it?

Lane reached out her hand to touch the big black trunk. At least she thought it had once been black. Now it was rust-colored, and the rust came off on her hands. The rust looked like dried blood, and she quickly pulled her hand back as if the trunk had bitten her. She reached out her hand again and discovered the trunk was open. There was just a very small slit of an opening, but it was enough that Lane could slide her hand inside and grab hold of the lid. She was not usually a big risk taker, and putting one's eleven-year-old hand inside a dirty dark hole of an ancient trunk was definitely risky. But her curiosity won out. She managed to lift the lid a little bit. The girls peered inside. It was dark, but when they opened the trunk a little more, the interior glittered, its golden secret shining in the summer sun. They saw a leather pouch that had ripped open. Hundreds of gold coins like the one Louisa had found that morning spilled out of the pouch. The girls gasped and their eyes got wide.

Lane was not quite speechless. "Louisa, this looks like real gold, a whole lot of real gold. Maybe we really have found a treasure!"

"I told you that coin I found was real money, but you didn't believe me."

Lane was willing to admit she'd made a mistake. "You were right. I really do think it's gold."

"The coins in these leather pouches are just like the ones I found in the sand this morning," Louisa was anxious to be vindicated.

Still sitting deep within their hole, they struggled with the lid, and together pulled it back so they could see what else was inside the chest. Lane pulled out a package of what looked like dollar bills. This part of the treasure was green-back paper money wrapped in yellowed cellophane bundles and tied with leather strips. When they picked up the packets of money, the leather strips fell apart in their hands. They saw lots more leather pouches in the trunk, and underneath them were stacks of small gold bars. Lane picked up a gold bar. It felt cool and heavy in her hands. She looked out at the ocean. The tide was coming in. Somehow she and Louisa would have to move their treasure because if they didn't, it would soon be covered with water. The girls had spent every summer of their lives playing in the sand on this Delaware beach. They understood the incoming tides and had seen sand castles, plastic pails and shovels, and even beach chairs disappear into the sea when left too close to the shore line.

Louisa noticed the tide too. "We need to put all of this treasure someplace safe. We have to rescue it before the tide comes in and takes it back out to sea." Louisa didn't think Lane was moving fast enough.

"We have to talk to our parents about it, Louisa, but you're right. First we need to get it out of this hole. You and I can't move the trunk by ourselves. It's too heavy, and it's old and rusty and looks like it might fall apart anyway," Lane was both excited and a little bit frightened by the find, but she was still thinking clearly. "My dad is asleep, and he gets mad when I wake him up. I don't know what time high tide is, but the water is coming in now. I'm afraid the water will fill up the hole before dinnertime."

"We need to move the treasure right now, but we need something bigger than these buckets," Louisa was thinking about what to do. She always had a practical solution to a problem. "I saw some cloth bags in the bunk room. You know, the kind with a drawstring? We can fill up the bags and take them to the house. The big plastic container under my bed is empty because my mom just took my clothes to Cece." When Louisa outgrew her clothes, her mom stored them in a plastic container under her bunk bed at the beach. When a nice pile of outgrown shorts, shirts, and other things had accumulated, Louisa's mom recycled them by giving them to a friend who had a younger daughter.

Lane decided to go along with Louisa's idea. "Okay, you run up to the house and get bigger bags. I'll stay here and guard the treasure." The discovery of the trunk seemed partly real and partly pretend to Lane.

Lane knew they had discovered something important, something about which the adults needed to be consulted. She also knew they had a limited amount of time before their hole in the sand and everything in it was filled with water and then washed out to sea. She told Louisa to hurry with the bags.

Louisa started out toward the wooden steps carrying a pink plastic sand bucket filled with gold coins from the trunk. She had scattered a few shells on top of the coins in case anybody looked at what was in her bucket. If anybody stopped her and asked her what she was doing, she planned to say she was just going up to the beach house to go to the bathroom. She went in the back door of the bunk room and didn't see anybody. She pulled the plastic container out from under her bed and dumped the coins from her plastic pail into the container. She found an old beach bag in the closet and another cloth shopping bag. Louisa ran to the beach with the empty bags. The girls quickly filled them with the contents of the trunk. The bags were too heavy for Louisa to carry two at the same time, so Lane decided she should be the one to make the trips to the house while Louisa stood guard over their cache. The bags were a challenge for Lane. She had to drag them along the sand and the wooden walkway to the beach house. The bags were so loaded with treasure she had to carry each one separately up the stairs to the house.

After several more trips, the girls had accomplished their mission. The plastic container under Louisa's bed couldn't hold all the coins and gold bars, so they had to store some of their bounty in the bottom drawer of the dresser in the closet. At the very bottom of the trunk, they found papers that didn't look very valuable. But the girls decided to try to save everything. After the tide came in, it would all be gone.

Lane had looked into one of the leather pouches, and she thought she'd seen a gun in the bag. Chills ran down her spine, and she had a sick feeling in her stomach. What would her mother say? How angry would she be that Lane had not asked her for help?

Lane and Louisa rescued the last contents of the trunk just as the sea water began to pour over the sides of their hole. The rusted, empty trunk was still in the hole and the girls did their best to drag it out of the hole and across the sand. It was battered and it was breaking into pieces. Louisa thought they should leave the trunk to the tides, but Lane insisted it might be "evidence." They carried the pieces they could salvage, including the lid of the trunk, which remained in one piece, and decided to bury it all beside the dune fence. They didn't have much time to dig a deep hole, but they managed to rescue the remains of the trunk and cover it over with sand. They hoped their quick work would be sufficient to keep it temporarily hidden. They were exhausted after their labors, and both were nervously wondering how they would tell their mothers about what they had done. When Lane thought about the gun in a bag that was now under Louisa's bed, she was downright terrified about what her mother would say. Her mother hated guns.

– Chapter Two –

By the Sea

1939

Elizabeth Darling James was eccentric. Her friends could think of no other way to describe the woman. As the years passed, the more unusual her lifestyle became, and at fifty-three, she was downright odd. What she was about to do was completely out of the ordinary, but it made complete sense to her. Her detractors thought she was out of her mind, even crazy, but she was too smart and too organized to be dismissed like that. Her children were grown and had moved away from the family home in Washington, D.C., and her husband Grayson had died some years ago. The house was too big for one woman and two dogs, so she decided to move and live full time in Bethany Beach, Delaware. Her family had spent many happy summer vacations there. Elizabeth had always loved the ocean, and she loved it in all of its seasons. Bethany was a popular summer resort, but in 1939 not very many people chose to live in houses at the beach during the chilly fall and cold winter months.

Elizabeth had long imagined herself living by the sea, and at last she was going to realize her dream. She was making plans to buy an oceanfront plot of land and build a house on it when an acquaintance told her about a cottage for sale south of the Indian River Inlet and north of Bethany Beach. The house was well-built, but older and needed work.

Elizabeth drove to the beach in Delaware to look at Rose Cottage. The moment she laid eyes on the weathered, gray-shingled house above the dunes, Elizabeth fell in love with it. She knew it had to be her home. In June, Elizabeth would discover to her great delight that *rosa rugosa*, the wild rose bushes that grow in abundance close to the ocean and thrive in the salt air, encircled her cottage with a fabulous display of pink and red.

One of Elizabeth's friends thought she had gone completely over the edge. "Why in the world would you want to do something like this?" she asked Elizabeth. "You have a wonderful life here in Washington. I know it's different for you since Grayson died, but you still get invited to lots of parties. Everybody still loves you."

Elizabeth smiled and sighed. She wondered if any of her friends would ever really understand. "I'm moving because I want to live someplace where, every morning for the rest of my life, the first thing I see when I wake up is the ocean. To spend my days overlooking sand dunes and rushing waves seems like the perfect way to spend my time."

When they heard her D.C. home was on the market and that she'd already bought a house near Bethany Beach, Elizabeth's friends knew things were serious and became even more concerned. They thought she was depressed and not thinking clearly. Why would Elizabeth do something so impulsive, so rash? Two of her closest friends invited her to join them for afternoon tea at the Willard Hotel. They knew she loved tea at the Willard—especially the scones—and thought they might be able to cheer her up or talk her out of her foolhardy decision. Arabella Hamilton Adams and Lady

Larmore Dudley arrived early and were seated at the low table when Elizabeth arrived. She gave them both air kisses and joined them on the settee.

"You look wonderful in that pink suit, dear," Arabella remarked. "Why anybody ever said red heads shouldn't wear pink hasn't seen you in a pink suit." Arabella always wanted to say something that would please, but what came out of her mouth was sometimes all wrong. That was one reason Elizabeth liked Arabella.

"My hair is hardly red anymore, and I'm wearing pink all the time these days because I've just bought a house called Rose Cottage." Elizabeth knew her friends had invited her to tea today to talk about her decision to move away from D.C., so she gave them the chance to get right to the point.

"Yes, Elizabeth Darling, we want to talk to you about that." Lady Larmore wasn't one to beat around the bush. Sometimes she was blunt to the point of being rude. She didn't mind telling people the truth, even though hearing the truth made some people uncomfortable. Her directness was one reason Elizabeth liked Lady Larmore.

When they first met, Elizabeth had asked Lady Larmore if she were royalty. Lady Larmore laughed and said, "You know, everybody wonders that when they first meet me, and everybody wants to ask me that question. But nobody has ever had the nerve to mention it the first time I've been introduced to them—except for you. Bravo! I think we are going to be great friends." They did become great friends. Lady Larmore was from Mississippi, and she explained to Elizabeth that "Lady" was considered to be a first name in the South. Southern women were often called by two names. Lady Larmore's two best friends from childhood were Mary Rose and Bettyrose Grace. Lady Larmore decided she would call her new friend Elizabeth Darling and had been calling Elizabeth by her first and middle names for more than twenty-five years.

"Tell me you aren't planning to live at the beach all year around." Lady Larmore couldn't imagine a house without central heating. "I understand you might not want to rattle around in that huge place now that your kids are grown and gone, but you could have a very nice apartment with a doorman in that new building on Connecticut Avenue."

"I'm going to live in Rose Cottage all year around, and I'm looking forward to the fall and winter months especially."

Arabella, who was always worrying about her own health and the health of others, said, "But those beach houses aren't heated, Elizabeth, and the kitchens are deplorable. One summer I rented a beach house on the Delaware Coast, and Jemma left after two days. She called her brother, and he drove down from D.C. and took her back home." Jemma was Arabella's cook. "Who will cook for you? Lena is way too old to live at the beach." Lena had been Elizabeth's cook since she'd married Grayson.

Elizabeth sipped her cup of tea and took an almond scone and a current scone from the tiered tray the waiter brought to the table. She covered the almond one with clotted cream, took a bite, and closed her eyes with pleasure. "Lena is retiring and going to live with her cousin in Barbados. I envy her the sunshine. Barbados is beautiful, and she is thrilled to be moving there. As for my house in Bethany Beach, of course I'm having it winterized. I'm putting in a heating system and all new windows. The house will be airtight, and I'll be snug as a bug when winter comes. And, I'm having a brand new kitchen and pantry wing built onto the house. It will have all the latest appliances—including my pride and joy, a six-burner Magic Chef Propane gas stove. It's expensive, but it's worth it. I will be doing all of my own cooking."

"We always thought you did that cooking thing just to show off for the men. Are you saying now that you really like to cook?" Cooking was a mystery to Arabella, and she was in awe of anyone who could actually put a meal on the table.

Arabella's comment annoyed Elizabeth. "When have you ever known me to do something just to show off for the men? For goodness sakes, Arabella, you know me better than that."

Lady Larmore was anxious to ask her own questions. "I know you've always liked renovating houses and fixing them up. You're very good at remodeling and decorating. I hope you're doing everything possible to make the house livable and comfortable. Does it have more than one bathroom? I would consider visiting you, but if there's only one bathroom, I will have to stay at a hotel." Lady Larmore was into fashion and make up. She'd had special lights installed around her bathroom mirror, like the kind the stars in Hollywood have in their dressing rooms.

Elizabeth wanted to reassure Lady Larmore that there would be plenty of indoor plumbing in her new home. "I added two wings to the house. One is the kitchen wing and the other is a large first floor bedroom with a completely modern bathroom—including an enormous claw foot tub. I've screened in the porch and installed a bed that hangs from the ceiling." Her two friends looked puzzled as if they were trying to imagine what that would look like and why anyone would want one. "It's for taking naps on summer afternoons and sleeping when the nights are too hot to sleep indoors. And, oh, I had my carpenter build me an enclosed outside shower on the first floor. You know how handy that is at the beach." Both her friends had rented beach houses during the summer months and knew how important an outside shower was for everyone.

"You know, Elizabeth Darling, the Cadillac will rust right through parked at the beach. I assume your house is up on pilings and you don't have a garage. Arthur says the salt air can rust through the undercarriage of a car in one winter—whatever an undercarriage is. Your roadster is so luxurious. I hate to see it ruined." Lady Larmore was savvy about financial matters and knew the Cadillac would lose its value if it were allowed to rust.

"I'm selling the Cadillac," Elizabeth told them. "It would never be the right thing to drive at the beach. My driveway from Route 1 to the house is dirt and gravel. A hard rain turns it into a sea of mud. I need a much more practical vehicle, so I've decided to buy a Ford pickup truck."

Elizabeth waited to see how her well-bred friends would react to the idea of a pickup truck. She wasn't disappointed when Arabella gasped and Lady Larmore, usually a woman with a lot to say, could only summon, "Oh, my!"

"A truck will take me everywhere I need to go—to the stores in Ocean View to buy groceries and hardware and to Salisbury, Maryland for special shopping and doctors' appointments. I'll park it under the house."

The women turned their attention to the tea sandwiches and pastries. After giving their friend the third degree, they all needed sustenance. Elizabeth had a second cup of lapsang suchong. Arabella liked Earl Gray, and Lady Larmore always brought her own custom home blend of herbal teas. The staff at the Willlard was very accommodating and brewed Lady Larmore's special tea for her. The women talked of family and neighbors and things other than Elizabeth's drastic lifestyle change and the fact that they would miss their quirky friend when she left Washington, D.C.

Arabella was not ready to let it go. "You have always been such a sociable person, Elizabeth. You did so much for your children's school, and you've been incredibly generous with your time doing volunteer work. I know a lot of those social events and dinner parties were necessary because of Grayson's position, and you were such a good sport about it.

I always wondered where you found the energy to do so much entertaining. But won't you be terrible lonely, living all by yourself like that? You don't know a soul. Is that a smart thing to do?" Arabella was a bit of a scaredy-cat. "From the way you've described Rose Cottage, you don't really have any close neighbors you could call on if you needed help."

"I chose Rose Cottage because of its isolation and magnificent ocean views," Elizabeth patiently responded. "I'm looking forward to a different kind of life. I want to sail my small sailboat on the inland bays. I love to swim in the ocean, and every day the water is warm enough, I'm going to swim. I've always wanted to paint, but never had the time. Raising four children doesn't leave much time or energy to indulge one's dreams. I'm not afraid to live alone, and I can take care of myself. And besides, I have a shotgun, and I know how to use it." Four wide eyes stared back at her. Their husbands hunted geese and ducks in Easton and St. Michaels, but the thought of Elizabeth wielding a shotgun was almost more than her friends could imagine.

Arabella's voice was a whisper, "Will you keep the shotgun loaded?"

"Of course, the shotgun will be loaded. What good would it be to me if I didn't keep it loaded?"

Lady Larmore had recovered her composure and had one last thought on her mind. "Please tell me you will have a telephone in your house. Elizabeth Darling, you are an older woman living alone, and even if you do keep a loaded shotgun in the house, you have to be able to call for help. Furthermore, I want to be able to call you and talk, even if it is long distance."

Elizabeth laughed at Lady Larmore's concern. "I do still have my wits about me, you know. It wasn't easy, but I have had a phone line installed. You know how a summer thunderstorm can take the phone lines down in a minute. I insisted that that the phone line from the road to the house be buried rather than installed above ground on a telephone poll the way they usually do it. The Diamond State Telephone Company didn't want to do it my way. They charged me a lot of money, but in the end I got what I wanted. I don't use the telephone very often, but I look forward to hearing my children's voices on Sunday evenings. I also got the local electric company to bury my electric line, rather than put it on a pole. Of course, they didn't want to do that either, and they also charged me a lot of money."

Lady Larmore sighed. "Well, it seems as if you've thought of everything. I'm somewhat relieved to hear about all of this. I will worry about you, though. You are very independent. You always have been, but this move comes as a shock to all of us."

"I know it's hard for you to understand why I've chosen to live my life in an unconventional way. Rose Cottage has plenty of room, and I hope you'll both come and visit me." Elizabeth wanted to make her friends feel better and hoped they would understand at least a little. "Bethany Beach is not that far away. Really, I'll be fine. I'll be happy in my cottage by the sea."

By the Beautiful Sea

— Chapter Three —

1939

In the early spring of 1939, Elizabeth sold the twenty-five room mansion on Massachusetts Avenue where she had raised her children and been the perfect hostess. She got rid of most of her furniture and stored what she couldn't use. She gave away closets full of clothes she'd worn in her former life as a grande dame of Washington D.C. society. One benefit of life at the beach was that she would never have to wear another evening gown or another pair of gloves that came above her elbows.

Elizabeth and her two dogs Licorice and Vanilla moved to Bethany Beach to live in Rose Cottage. They gloried in the sunshine and the blue water of the Atlantic Ocean. Elizabeth often wondered, as she was making her new life, what her deceased husband Grayson James would have thought of her decision to move to Bethany Beach. Elizabeth had graduated from Smith College and had earned a master's degree in history from the University of Pennsylvania before her marriage, so Grayson had known from the beginning he was dealing with a smart woman who had a mind of her own.

Grayson was a widower who fell head over heels in love with the young, energetic staffer who worked at the Department of the Navy. He couldn't resist the red head with bright blue eyes and a big smile. They met at a cocktail party at the Belgian Embassy. Elizabeth was swept off her feet by the very handsome and very rich older man. During the almost thirty years they lived and laughed together in their Washington home, Elizabeth gave birth to two boys and two girls who were now adults with families of their own.

Elizabeth was very aware of geopolitical events and the twists and turns of economics and history. She may have decided to embrace the eccentric side of herself, but she was still a very bright woman who understood what was happening in the world. What was happening in the world in 1939 was not good. Even as she was excited and happy about her new home and her new life, Elizabeth worried about her country and the countries in Europe which shared the precious democratic values of the United States. In her younger days, she had traveled extensively throughout Europe and the world accompanying her husband on diplomatic missions, and she was sickened by the news currently coming out of Germany. She imagined that whatever was really happening in that sad place was much worse than anyone really knew.

No one wanted to believe that war was the only solution to even the worst problems, but Elizabeth was not alone in her fear that war might be the only way to bring down the Nazi scourge. She was filled with dread when she considered what the implications of another war would be for her own family and for the world. She was glad that Grayson was not alive to see another war. She could never put her concerns about what was happening overseas completely out of her mind, but she knew that life was short and wanted to experience as much of its joy as she could. Moving to Rose Cottage was one of the ways Elizabeth had chosen to embrace her own happiness.

Rose Cottage was protected by the twenty-five acres of property Elizabeth had purchased with the house and by a vast tract of adjacent land owned by the State of Delaware. Elizabeth had invested in this large piece of real estate primarily to prevent potential neighbors from building close to her and obscuring her views. Although she was usually quite frugal, Elizabeth had plenty of money and didn't mind spending it to make her new and simpler lifestyle the way she wanted it to be.

On this rainy Monday morning, Elizabeth's miniature Scottish terrier, Licorice, was trying to hide behind the couch, thinking his mistress wouldn't notice. Licorice didn't like to go out in the rain. Vanilla, Elizabeth's West Highland terrier, didn't like the rain either, but she knew better than to try to fool Elizabeth. "Don't try to sneak away and hide from me, Licorice," Elizabeth reached for the little black dog's red collar. "You know we never miss our morning walk, no matter what the weather is like." Elizabeth's new morning routine began with a walk on the beach accompanied by her dogs. Elizabeth was devoted to her dogs. They went everywhere with her.

Elizabeth and the dogs donned their raingear. Elizabeth thought dogs looked silly in raincoats, but their hair was so long and got so wet when they were out in the rain, she'd had the raincoats specially made for them. She also had winter coats for them to wear when the temperature plummeted. Both dogs liked to play in the snow and didn't mind the cold. Licorice and Vanilla loved the beach and chased the tufts of foam the ocean waves tossed up on the sand.

After their morning constitutional, Elizabeth and the dogs ate breakfast. She made dog food from her own recipe, and the dogs refused to eat anything else. Elizabeth had yogurt and whatever fruit was in season for breakfast in warm weather. Sometimes she added a piece of whole wheat toast.

When the weather got cold, she would eat a bowl of stone ground oatmeal with brown sugar and heavy cream.

After breakfast, Elizabeth began her chores. She changed the sheets on her bed, vacuumed and dusted the house, and cleaned her bathroom. She did the little bit of laundry that required hand washing and hung it up to dry. She hung her clothes outside if the weather were nice, and she hung them inside if the weather were cold or rainy. The laundry that she didn't do herself, she took to a laundress in Clarksville, Delaware. Elizabeth had been fortunate to have servants take care of these things for her when she was living an upper-class life in the city, but now she enjoyed the two hours of housework required to keep her small cottage spic and span.

Tomorrow she would run her errands. The dogs always rode with her in the truck when she drove into town. Every Tuesday she bought her groceries, went to the hardware store and the post office, and did whatever shopping and business were required to keep her simple life in order. She always made a trip to the dairy farm owned by a Mennonite family where she bought her milk and cream, eggs, yogurt, and sour cream. When it was available, she bought egg custard that was Mrs. Adkins' specialty. The matron who ran the farm always had treats for the dogs, so they, too, loved to visit the Mennonite farm.

At a beach house there is always sand on the floor that needs to be swept. It is a never ending task. Elizabeth wondered, as she swept the ubiquitous sand into a dustpan, if it were raining in D.C. today and what her children were doing. They had been upset when she'd told them she was moving to Bethany Beach. They understood why she wanted to sell the house which was much too large for a woman living alone, and they tried to talk her into buying a smaller place in the D.C. area. But her children knew their mother, and when they realized how determined she was to live at the beach, they supported her decision to buy Rose Cottage. Each of them had been down to see the place for themselves, and they all had to admit it was lovely. They could see their independent mother living there on the dunes with her dogs. They would miss her very much, but they promised to visit often. Elizabeth told them she would write to them regularly and tell them in detail all about her adventurous new life.

When it was cool outside, Elizabeth built a fire and sat at her desk by the window where she could watch the waves break on the shore as she wrote long letters to her children every week, paid bills, and took care of her household accounts. Elizabeth shared with her family what she had done the previous week, how she was managing, and how much she loved life at the beach. She didn't want to make them feel excluded, but she did want them to know she was content.

Elizabeth liked to eat lunch promptly at noon and had a sandwich and a salad made from the greens in her garden. Almost every day, she took a one-hour nap after lunch. Because it was cool and damp today she dozed on the very comfortable sofa in front of her fireplace. After her nap, she decided today was a day for painting rather than sailing or gardening. Elizabeth had joined the Rehoboth Art League and was devoting more and more time to her painting.

At five o'clock she took the dogs to the beach for another long walk. The weather had begun to clear, and when the threesome returned, Elizabeth fed her dogs and cooked a full dinner of meat, potatoes, two vegetables, and dessert for herself. When the weather was nice, she ate on her porch overlooking the ocean. When winter came she would enjoy her dinner on the small drop leaf table in front of a crackling fire.

Elizabeth spent the evening listening to music on the radio, and she was always reading one or two books. After soaking in a long, relaxing bubble bath, Elizabeth lifted the dogs onto her canopy bed. The bed was one of the few pieces of furniture she had brought with her from her former life. She'd fitted out the canopy with yards of mosquito netting which she used in the summer so she could keep her windows open in hot weather. She had screens on the windows, but the pesky flies and mosquitoes knew how to get through the smallest holes. If it was really hot, she slept in her suspended bed which hung on the screened porch. She read her mystery novel until her eyelids grew heavy, and as she drifted off to sleep, she listened to the ocean waves crashing on the shore.

The week of rainy weather was unusual for July, and by the weekend, Elizabeth was ready to see the sun and clear skies. She liked to do something different and fun on Saturday, although in reality she felt that every moment of her new life was fun. She thought about driving to Chincoteague, Virginia to attend a seafood festival but decided it was too far. She also considered going to the sidewalk art exhibit in Lewes, Delaware or making the trip to Rehoboth Beach to eat lunch or have dinner in a favorite restaurant. Because it was a beautiful day, Elizabeth packed a lunch, put Licorice and Vanilla on the sailboat, and spent the day letting the wind show her the way. Cold weather would be here soon enough, and she would no longer be able to take her boat out on the water. When the temperature began to drop, she would spend her Saturday afternoons listening to the opera on her shortwave radio.

On Sunday morning Elizabeth and her dogs drove to Bethany Beach to attend church services at the Episcopal Church. The dogs waited in the truck. Elizabeth did whatever she felt like doing on Sunday afternoons. Sometimes she threw sticks for her dogs, weeded her vegetable garden, or pruned the wild *rosa rugosa* that grew in magnificent profusion around her cottage. Sometimes, she read or worked on a crossword puzzle. Sometimes she took a long nap. Today she just sat on the beach and watched the ocean.

Elizabeth finished washing the few dinner dishes and closed her kitchen for the evening. An afternoon thunderstorm had brought an end to the fair weather, and it had started raining again. The dogs were waiting for her in the living room. When the weather was fine, they sat on the porch after dinner. Just as she was about to join her canine pals on the couch, the phone rang. It was so loud, she almost jumped out of her skin. The phone hardly ever rang, and it always startled her when she heard it. She kept the phone on her desk in the living room and hurried to answer.

"Hello! Hello! Is this Elizabeth Darling James?" Before Elizabeth could respond, the voice continued. "How silly of me. Of course it is. Who else would it be unless you've taught Licorice or Vanilla to answer the phone? Hello, Elizabeth Darling. This is Lady Larmore Dudley calling you."

"Oh, Lady Larmore, it's wonderful to hear from you. I recognized your voice immediately. Is everything all right?" Elizabeth always worried, when somebody called long distance unexpectedly, that it might be bad news.

"I've missed you, Elizabeth Darling. So tell me, dear, how are you and what in the world are you doing with yourself? Do you sit on the beach all day? Are you really cooking?"

"I walk on the beach every day, but I hardly ever just sit there. And yes, I am cooking. I planted a garden, you know. I grow herbs and vegetables – parsley, basil, chives, rosemary, the usual suspects. I had all kinds of salad greens earlier in the spring, and now I'm harvesting tomatoes, green beans, watercress, and eggplant."

"What do you do with all that food?" Lady Larmore wouldn't have any idea what to do with food that didn't arrive already prepared on her plate.

"I've bought a canner and dozens of jars, and I'm going to can tomatoes and green beans. I buy peaches and plums from the farm stands along the road and freeze the fruit. I'm canning and freezing now because there is so much wonderful fresh produce. After the garden is finished for the year, I will bake bread and make soup."

"Do you still make your wonderful spaghetti sauce? I know you do."

"Oh, yes, I've been making the spaghetti sauce with fresh tomatoes and basil, and then I preserve the sauce in glass jars. I'm having a wonderful time playing with my new stove and my new canner."

"Wait until I tell everyone you have turned into Betty Crocker or Fanny Farmer or somebody." Lady Larmore always liked to be the one with the latest news.

Elizabeth had a confession to make to her friend. "You know, I may actually have turned into one of those. I've always liked to sew, and now I'm making my own clothes. I order fabric from that store on G Street."

"You never stop surprising me. Do you look at all presentable in homemade clothes? I shudder at the thought. And please tell me you don't make your own underwear or your own shoes."

Elizabeth laughed. She decided Lady Larmore could handle one more confession of domesticity. "I've also taken up knitting and have gotten pretty good at it."

"Knitting? What do you knit? Hats and scarves?"

"Yes, I knit those, but I also knit my own sweaters and sweaters for the dogs."

"Sweaters for the dogs? To wear under their raincoats?" Lady Larmore also thought dogs looked silly in raincoats.

"You always make me laugh, dear friend. I do miss you." Elizabeth enjoyed Lady Larmore's humor and sarcasm and really did miss her friend.

"Please don't ever let Arthur know you're doing all of this cooking and canning and whatnot. I'm certainly not going to tell him. He might get the idea that I ought to take a page from your cookbook and start to be domestic. Of course, he knows that will never happen. In fact, before he left on this latest trip abroad, I was very out of sorts because he had a new project in mind for me."

"Arthur had a project for you?" Elizabeth knew that Arthur knew better than to try to plan Lady Larmore's time for her.

"He became obsessed with our basement. Can you imagine? He kept talking about the basement and asking me what was down there, although he knows very well I have no idea what's in the basement. I've never been down there. Why would I want to go into the basement? The servants do that sort of thing."

"What do you mean he became obsessed with your basement?" Elizabeth knew that Lady Larmore sometimes got odd ideas into her head, but there was usually something behind it. She couldn't figure out where Lady Larmore was headed this time.

Lady Larmore continued, "He actually went down into the basement himself and spent an hour or more doing God knows what. I though he had lost his mind and couldn't imagine what he'd found that was so interesting. When he came back upstairs, he wanted to talk to me about cleaning it out. He said he wanted me to get the basement cleaned out while he was on this trip to Europe. Can you imagine, me cleaning out the basement? Well, I set him straight on that."

Elizabeth laughed, "I'm sure you did, Lady Larmore."

"He said he hadn't meant that I ought to clean it out myself, but that I should find somebody to do it. I asked him why he was so interested in the basement all of a sudden, and he told me it would keep us safe if we were attacked from the air. Then I was sure he had lost his mind. I asked him what in the world he meant by a remark like that. I asked him who he thought was going to attack us from the air. Then he started to get cagy --- you know how he gets when he doesn't want to talk about something."

Elizabeth knew exactly what Arthur was concerned about, but she was surprised he was taking it so seriously this summer. "He's thinking way ahead, Lady Larmore. He's planning for what he hopes will never happen. Lots of people think there's going to be a war. Everyone in Washington must be talking about that."

"When Arthur got quiet and decided he wasn't going to discuss the basement any more, I told him I knew what was going on in the world. I told him I knew there was going to be a war but it wouldn't involve the United States. He gave me a hard look and said something about the Yanks getting into it sooner or later. Why would he want to scare me like that?"

"Lady Larmore, I think Arthur was just trying to be honest with you. Nobody wants to think about going to war again, but it's better to be prepared than to put one's head in the sand."

"That's exactly what Arthur told me, and he said he wanted the basement to be cleaned out by the time he came home from this trip. I've got my household help working on it, and I've hired people to haul things away. It's not exactly the way I'd hoped to spend my summer."

"Good for you! Are you almost done?" Elizabeth was impressed that her friend had been able to supervise an undertaking as sizeable and as domesticated as the basement cleanout.

"Yes, it's almost done. I guess I should be glad Arthur only wanted me to get the basement cleaned out. Imagine if he'd expected me to buy a canner and learn to use it. Ha! Ha! He would never suggest that. He wouldn't have the nerve." Lady Larmore knew her limitations and would much rather hear about Elizabeth's life in the kitchen than to think of doing it herself.

Lady Larmore was suddenly quiet, and Elizabeth knew there was something her friend wanted to say but didn't quite know how. "Tell me what you're doing, Lady Larmore. Are you still coming to the beach next month?"

"Everything is lovely ... well, really it isn't, truth be told, my dear," Lady Larmore hesitated again. "As a matter of fact, that's one of the reasons I called. You know, I'd written that we had rented a house in Lewes for the month of August. I was so looking forward to seeing you, and the house sounded quite nice. It even came with a staff of three, but that's beside the point now. One of the reasons I'm calling is to tell you we aren't coming in August. Arthur was scheduled to be home at the end of July, and now he's sent me a cable from Warsaw to say he's not coming home until further notice – whatever that means. I told him I was going to Lewes with or without him. He was adamant that I not go. I insisted he tell me why, and he refused. Something's going on, Elizabeth Darling. Something is definitely going on. Lady Larmore's voice dropped to a whisper, "Arthur's a spook, you know." Elizabeth laughed because her friend could be so frank. Before Elizabeth could say a word, Lady Larmore continued, whispering as if she were afraid someone else besides Elizabeth could hear her. "I think it's all right to tell you about his being a spook because you don't live in D.C. any more. Arthur tells everyone he works for the Navy Department, but everybody knows he's a spook. He's the only one who thinks it's a secret."

Elizabeth was still chuckling, "I'd suspected for a long time that he was working as a spy for Naval Intelligence, but I don't see why you had to cancel your trip to Lewes."

"Tomorrow is my birthday, and he's not going to be home for that either, of course. It's not the end of the world, but calling you long distance is the birthday present I'm giving to myself. He won't dare squawk when he gets the bill. He's feeling too guilty."

"Happy Birthday, Lady Larmore. I sent you a small gift. You should have it by now."

"Oh, yes, thank you so much. The postman brought it yesterday, but I haven't opened it yet. I'm saving it to open tomorrow. But I do want to tell you that Arabella and I and several of your other friends met for tea at the Hay Adams yesterday, and we didn't talk about anything but you. You're on everybody's mind, and all of us are wondering what you're up to. We had lots of those lovely minced ham and sweet pickle sandwiches on brown bread --- the ones you like so much. That's what reminded us of you --- how much you love those tea sandwiches. The Hay Adams does such a lovely tea. Of course they had turkey salad with chutney and the cheese and tomato. All excellent as usual. The cheese and tomato are especially delicious when tomatoes are at their peak, but the cucumber sandwiches were not quite up to the usual standard. I think they are leaving the Lee & Perrins or the garlic out of the cream cheese, and it's just not as good. They did have a new lemon scone which we all loved and ate with blueberry jam."

"Lady Larmore, please stop. I've just finished dinner and you are making me hungry again. Oh, how I'd love to have a box of those minced ham sandwiches."

"You see, you do miss your old life here, and we miss you. I especially miss you. You were always a breath of fresh air in this stuffy town." Lady Larmore sounded lonely. "I'm so depressed I won't get to see you next month. Stay in touch. I'm very angry with Arthur right now, although I know he would come home if he could."

Lady Larmore paused, "I had the strangest letter from him last week. He asked me all sorts of questions about Cape Henlopen. He wanted me to find out exactly how many miles Cape Henlopen was from Lewes --- both as the crow flies and on the road. He wanted to know lots of things about exactly how to get to Fort Miles and what the roads are like. He has hundreds of maps in his study, and I spent an entire afternoon looking at the maps and measuring distances. I'm pretty good with a map, but he wanted so many details. Then he insisted I send him all of the information in a telegram, and he wanted it sent that day. It was so strange, Elizabeth Darling. I know bad things are happening in Europe, but what does Arthur have to do with it? He forgot to wish me happy birthday in his letter, so I know he's very preoccupied with something important. Anyway, I miss you. It sounds as if your life is peachy. Ha! Ha! Maybe I'll drive down one day and visit you. You promised me my own bathroom if I came to stay."

"I'd love it if you came to see me. Please do. It's been wonderful talking to you. Thanks for giving yourself this nice birthday gift. It was a gift to me as well. Take care of yourself, and I hope to see you in D.C. You know I don't go across the bay in the summer." In 1939, the only way to cross the Chesapeake Bay from Annapolis to Kent Island was to take the car ferry. The two-lane toll bridge across the bay was not completed until 1952.

"Yes, very smart. I'll for sure see you in the fall. Good bye, dear heart. Stay well."

Elizabeth had loved talking to her friend and had to admit to herself that she really did miss some things about her life in D.C. The next time she went to visit her family, she would go to the Hay Adams to try the lemon scones. Elizabeth loved afternoon tea and had found a place closer to home where she could indulge.

Elizabeth took the dogs out one more time. The phone call from Lady Larmore had both cheered and worried her. It was so unlike Arthur Dudley to insist that Lady Larmore cancel their vacation. He was usually the adventurous one and was game for almost anything. Lady Larmore was the one who wanted to be sure, whatever undertaking Dudley proposed, that there was always a place close by where she could get her hair done.

War was coming and it was coming soon. Elizabeth didn't have a crystal ball, but she paid attention. For years, she'd lived with a vague sense of foreboding that the world was turning dark. In the past few weeks, her fears for the future had become more immediate and more ominous. As she lay in bed listening to the waves, she was grateful she lived on this side of the Atlantic. Here in this place and safe for now, life was good for Elizabeth.

– Chapter Four –

The Winds of War

1939-1942

L ife was not good for the rest of the world in 1939. The threat of war was closing in on the countries across the Atlantic. Elizabeth had one carefree summer in her new home before the little Austrian tyrant turned Europe and all of civilization upside down. On September 1, 1939, Hitler invaded Poland, and World War Two began.

Two of Elizabeth's paintings had been chosen for the annual Labor Day sidewalk show in Lewes. She was surprised and flattered, especially since she was a novice painter. Elizabeth had driven to Lewes to see her work displayed. She couldn't believe it was already September first. Where had the summer gone?

After the art show, Elizabeth headed to the small Lewes tearoom where she was planning to enjoy a wonderful afternoon tea instead of fixing dinner. It was too hot to cook. The Seaside English Tearoom made delicious watercress and cream cheese sandwiches, and their smoky lapsang suchong tea was the best she'd ever tasted. The Seaside reminded Elizabeth of a tearoom she'd frequented when she was living in

London with her husband and children. She'd had an excellent British nanny there, and when they were at home, tea had been served every day at four in the afternoon. Elizabeth enjoyed her trip down memory lane that tea time in Lewes made possible. She promised herself that if she were ever blessed with a granddaughter, they would get dressed up, put on their hats and short white gloves, and drive to Lewes for a cream tea. They would order all the pastries on the menu. She hoped that day would come before too long.

Elizabeth was having her second cup of lapsang suchong and indulging in one of her favorite pastimes, people watching, when the bell on the tearoom door broke her reverie. Because of the time she had spent in England, Elizabeth knew immediately that the tall man who had just burst through the doorway was an admiral in the British Royal Navy. He was splendid in the dark blue uniform, and his military carriage caused everyone in the tearoom to stare at him. He was obviously agitated as he rushed to the table next to Elizabeth's. Something was terribly wrong, and Elizabeth was more than a little curious to know what could have put this distinguished man into such a state.

The admiral pulled out a chair from the table where his family was seated and enjoying their tea. Elizabeth could see his wife's face, and the woman looked alarmed and annoyed. Her husband was making a spectacle of himself with his noisy entrance and his lack of manners. Elizabeth strained to overhear what was being said between the proper British man and woman. The two well-dressed and well-behaved little girls were wide-eyed to see their father so upset.

"What on earth has gotten into you, Ambrose? You're very late, so we went ahead without you. The children were hungry."

"Hitler has invaded Poland. It happened just before five o'clock Warsaw time this morning. Poland will be crushed under the Nazi boot before the week is out." Ambrose was trying to keep his voice down, but his emotions were running high. Everyone in the Seaside Tearoom could hear him. Several people gasped, and Elizabeth dropped her spoon on the floor with a loud clatter. All eyes turned in the direction of the table where Ambrose was seated.

Nobody said anything. The nice English family was stunned. Within a few seconds the younger girl began to cry. "What will happen, Daddy? Will England go to war? Will we be able to go home, or will we have to stay in America forever?"

The child had asked her father the questions everyone was thinking. Elizabeth hurried to pay her bill. She wanted to go home to Rose Cottage. She wanted to walk on the sand with her dogs. She wanted to collect her thoughts and say some prayers. As she left, she stopped by the table where the admiral and his family were sitting, still too much in shock to converse with each other. Elizabeth put her hand on the wife's shoulder. "I lived in London for two years, and I love your country. Whatever happens in the months and years ahead, in the end, England will prevail. England will destroy this evil. I am as certain of that as I have ever been of anything." She smiled at the girls and wished the family Godspeed.

Elizabeth had a shortwave radio, and every night she sat huddled with Licorice and Vanilla and listened to the BBC report the terrible news. She was worried sick about the world, in spite of doing everything she could to remove herself from it.

Elizabeth knew the United States would eventually join the war, and the evidence indicated that her country was already in it. There were attempts to keep the extent of U.S. efforts under wraps, but Elizabeth and almost everybody else in the world knew what was really happening. Although she couldn't see them as they passed by, she knew that every day ships loaded with food and fuel, weapons, oil, and other things vital to the war effort were in the Atlantic Ocean just off shore heading north towards Newfoundland. The final destination of this lifeline of supplies was Great Britain. Without this enormous maritime effort, the Nazis would eventually overrun the British Isles.

Lady Larmore had told Elizabeth that British children received almost their entire supply of vitamin C from the citrus carried in freighters from Florida. Because war precluded importing citrus from other places, the American fruit that traveled north along the East Coast of the United States and then across the North Atlantic was critical to Great Britain. Vitamin C is vital to health and survival, and without it, children develop scurvy, a vitamin deficiency disease that irreparably stunts their growth and harms the normal development of their bones. Citrus fruit was one of countless critical products our Merchant Marine ships carried to our friends and allies across the pond.

Elizabeth had never heard of something called bauxite, but she learned that bauxite ore from South America, an essential ingredient in the manufacture of aluminum, moved through the Caribbean and up the Atlantic Coast of the United States. The aluminum would be used to build airplanes. Ships carrying other raw materials to support the war sailed along the East Coast of the United States. Iron, tin, concrete, phosphate, lumber, and cotton filled the holds of these merchant ships. Cargos of vegetables, sugar, coffee and other foodstuffs, which fed the British military and the civilian population, made the dangerous journey.

The United States supplied oil, that elixir on which every war ran, in tremendous quantities to the Allied cause. Great Britain alone consumed more than four tankers' worth of oil each day. Elizabeth knew these tankers full of crude oil traveled along the East Coast day and night. One of their destinations was the complex of refineries that operated in and around Philadelphia where oil was converted into gasoline to power airplanes, tanks, trucks, and other vehicles of war. These oil tankers, on their way to Philadelphia, had to pass by Cape Henlopen at the mouth of the Delaware River.

Elizabeth watched with curiosity as fortifications, in the form of cement observation towers, were constructed along the beaches in Delaware from Cape Henlopen to Fenwick Island. Although no one was willing to give her an official reason for these "fire control towers," eleven of them would eventually be built to protect and defend United States beaches and waterways, as well as the ships that sailed along the Atlantic Coast. Elizabeth heard from a friend who had recently visited Cape May that similar towers were being built along the beaches of southern New Jersey.

Located on relatively empty stretches of the shore, the towers were erected in part to prevent the enemy from mobilizing along the beaches, as the allies would do in 1944 during the invasion of Normandy. The observation towers were built just behind the dunes to serve as lookout posts for enemy surface ships. They were positioned to make use of triangulation techniques that could pinpoint a ship's location at sea. Being able to precisely locate enemy ships would make it possible to accurately direct the firing of big guns during an attack. Military and civilian volunteers and women and men of all ages and walks of life from nearby towns watched from these lookout posts for ships and enemy invaders.

As too often happens when preparing for the next war, military experts later realized that those who had conceived the idea for and made the decision to build these towers had made a classic military mistake. Armies and navies are always fighting the last war, and surface ships would not be the menace the Americans feared. German U-boats would be the greatest danger to shipping off the Mid-Atlantic Coast. At the time, no one could have predicted the bloodbath Germany was planning for the coastal waters of the United States.

Cape Henlopen, where the Delaware Bay empties into the Atlantic Ocean, has a unique and critical geographical position. Located at the point where tankers leave the dangers of the open ocean and gain the safety of a United States inland waterway, Cape Henlopen was the only possible place to prevent invading German ships and U-boats from entering the Delaware River. Facilities of strategic importance to the war effort could be accessed through the Delaware Bay, and it was vital that no enemy submarines be allowed to enter those waters. Industries in Wilmington, Delaware, the Naval Shipyard in Philadelphia, and oil refineries in both New Jersey and Pennsylvania had to be protected at all costs. It was unthinkable that a U-boat might be able to travel undetected up the Delaware River and bring destruction to these critical sites. Guarding the mouth of the Delaware River became a priority. The towers along the Delaware beaches were part of the fortification system designed to keep the country and its refining and shipbuilding capabilities safe.

Elizabeth liked to go to the Cape Henlopen area, which had been known as the "Cape Henlopen Lighthouse Reservation" before it was turned over to the United States War Department in 1938. Elizabeth drove her truck or rode her bicycle all around the dunes and dirt roads. Cape Henlopen, with its pristine beaches and its matchless view of the water, was one of the first locations in the New World to be established as a public land use area. William Penn, for whom the state of Pennsylvania is named, declared in 1682 that the more than five thousand acres around Cape Henlopen be set aside for the "usage of the citizens of Lewes and Sussex County." Elizabeth liked Cape Henlopen for its scenic beauty and enjoyed picnic lunches there with her dogs. Sometimes they fell asleep and napped for hours on a blanket.

The significant acreage at Cape Henlopen had been designated by the federal government as a military installation years before Fort Miles, at a cost of twenty-two million dollars, was constructed on that spot. Fort Miles was completed as an Army post in early December of 1941, just a few days before the surprise attack on the United State's Pacific Fleet at Pearl Harbor. The garrison at Fort Miles, which guarded the Delaware River, opened for military business within days of the United States' entry into World War Two.

As part of the Harbor Defense of Delaware, Fort Miles was strategic for both the United States Navy and the United States Army. It was not a large military facility and had not been at all secret or restricted before the war. Elizabeth heard that there were enormous superguns being installed at Fort Miles to guard the entrance to the Delaware Bay, and, all of a sudden, Fort Miles was off limits to everybody. There was a gatehouse with a barrier across the entrance. There were armed guards who checked IDs and papers and sent away anyone who did not have official business at the military site. More importantly, a controlled naval minefield to prevent enemy ships from entering the Delaware River estuary was also being constructed.

On December 7, 1941, the world changed for Elizabeth, as it changed for every American. Shortly after that infamous day, she heard from both of her sons that they were joining the U.S. Navy. One of her daughters, who was not yet married, had taken a job with Roosevelt's War Department in Washington, D.C. These choices did not surprise her. She would have expected no less from her patriotic children. In her heart of hearts she feared, as all mothers fear when their children go off to war, that they would not come home. She kept her fears and her sadness to herself and cheered them on in their brave decisions to fight for their country.

Elizabeth had lived at Rose Cottage for more than two years when her country declared war on Germany and Japan. She looked around and wondered how she could aid the war effort. The first thing she would do would be to volunteer to take a watch at the lookout towers all along the Delaware beachfront. Military professionals were in short supply these days, and volunteers had become a valuable commodity. She could knit bandages and suspected there would be plenty of demand for those in the months and years to come. She could certainly drive an ambulance if anybody in Bethany Beach needed one.

Elizabeth had lived through World War I in Washington D.C., but the United States had been involved in that conflict for a relatively short period of time. She was afraid this next war would be very different and much more costly in terms of treasure and in terms of lives. She grieved for the long days and nights of uncertainty for herself and for all those who were sending loved ones off to fight.

What Elizabeth never anticipated was that the war would arrive at her own front yard, and it would be sooner rather than later. The war, in the form of Germany's Operation Paukenschlag (Operation Drumbeat), came to the beaches of Delaware and to all the beaches along the East Coast of the United States in the winter of 1942.

Elizabeth knew that German U-boats in the North Atlantic had been terribly destructive to the British Navy and Merchant Marine ships that carried arms and materials of war from the United States across the ocean to our friends the Brits. Convoys had been heading to Britain via Newfoundland since 1939. She'd heard on her shortwave radio about the courage of the Royal Air Force as those brave airmen fought the Battle of Britain. She also heard the news about the destruction of hundreds of military ships and civilian mercantile transport vessels by the infamous wolf packs, groups of German U-boats in the North Atlantic. She had not expected, as no one had, that the German U-boat threat would come to her very own beach.

The United States had scarcely entered the war against Germany when the attacks began off the Eastern Seaboard. Germany brought the fight to the shores of the USA on January 11, 1942, with their first U-boat attack on a U.S. ship off the Atlantic Coast, and they were relentless. From January through August of 1942, German U-boats off the Atlantic Coast destroyed more than 400 freighters and tankers. Thousands of civilian Merchant Mariners' lives were lost. The danger to commercial shipping was so severe that it threatened to sever Britain's lifeline. The United States Navy was slow to respond to the U-boat threat.

Elizabeth found it almost impossible to believe that the Germans were already at the shores of Bethany Beach, but the evidence was irrefutable. Elizabeth saw ships burning off the coast during those winter months of 1942. She listened to the radio to try to find confirmation of what was happening. She scoured the local newspapers and read the Washington and New York newspapers to try to find reports about the ships being sunk. She went to the post office and asked the supervisor if he knew what had been burning in the ocean. No one wanted to talk about what was taking place right in front of their eyes. Everyone wanted to pretend that the war was not being fought just a few hundred yards from the shoreline of the United States. Nobody wanted to talk about what they had seen or what they knew. The homeland was in serious denial.

Elizabeth continued her early morning walks with the dogs, a custom that rarely varied, no matter what the weather. Mistress and dogs put on their winter coats and walked in pouring rain, sleet, snow, and high winds. Once, Elizabeth had cancelled the morning walks for ten days in a row because she'd had a severe case of the flu that turned into pneumonia. Elizabeth was seldom sick and was quite annoyed when illness laid her low. Another time, she had cancelled the morning walks because of a hurricane.

One morning, after she had seen a ship burning off shore the night before, she was walking along the beach with Licorice and Vanilla and noticed debris floating on the water. It was too cold to wade out into the surf, although she considered doing that. Some of the wreckage had washed up on the beach, and Elizabeth could see it was scraps of burned clothing. Finding these damaged remnants, these clothes that living breathing human beings had been wearing just hours earlier, brought home to Elizabeth the horror of the enemy attacks against her country's ships. Why didn't anybody seem to care about what was happening? The evidence was everywhere, and everyone was pretending there was nothing to see.

Elizabeth even drove to Georgetown, Delaware to talk with the Sussex County Sheriff's Office about what she had witnessed. The deputy looked at her, while she was telling her story, as if he thought she were delusional. He brushed off her concerns as if he really didn't care what she had to say. Not very many people were living on the beach in the winter months, and Elizabeth wondered if maybe she were the only person who had actually seen ships burning. This made it even more important, from her point of view, for her to report what she had observed.

Where was the Coast Guard? Where was the United States Navy? Elizabeth still had a few connections in Washington D.C., and she intended to call someone she knew who was currently working in the Department of the Navy. That someone was Arthur Dudley, the husband of her good friend Lady Larmore Dudley. She would tell him what she had seen, what was happening in the Atlantic Ocean right in front of her house, and she would ask him what the U.S. Navy intended to do about it.

– Chapter Five –

The Second Happy Time

Spring 1942

Reinhard Hoffmann realized his days fighting the war on a U-boat were coming to an end. He would have received his own command by now if he'd not been badly wounded in the Battle of the North Atlantic. During that period, known to the Germans as The First Happy Time, groups of German U-boats called wolf packs, had destroyed military and civilian ships as they tried to reach Great Britain. Reinhard had loved fighting the British and sinking their convoys of arms and oil as they traveled from the United States.

Then his submarine had been hit, and he'd been lucky to escape with his life. Most of his fellow Kriegsmarine (Nazi Navy) comrades aboard the sinking U-boat had died in the attack. Reinhard had been rescued, transferred to a German destroyer, and given life-saving medical care. His left leg was badly wounded, but it was saved. He now walked with a significant limp that normally would have disqualified him for

further sea duty on any German Navy vessel. But Reinhard
had convinced an admiral friend of his father's that he could
continue his position as the chief supply officer on a U-boat.

Reinhard's family was in the banking business and had
been very well off before the war. Reinhard had grown up in
a fine house and received a first-rate education. His father had
died over the English Channel early in the war when his plane
was shot down by a British pilot during the Battle of Britain.
Reinhard was expected to take over the family businesses
and become the head of the family bank, but he preferred
military life and had happily delegated most of the duties of
the running of the bank and the businesses to others.

Reinhard was worried about the direction Germany was
taking in the war. He began to think about his own future
and decided he needed to have sizeable financial resources
that he could get to at a moment's notice. He helped himself
to some of the family bank's assets in the form of foreign
currencies, gold coins, and gold bars. The bank had access
to gold and cash from around the world. Reinhard kept his
purloined treasure buried in the garden of the family mansion
outside Dusseldorf.

Having completed courses of study in finance and military
history at the University of Heidelberg, Reinhard's position
in the German Navy was not yet commensurate with his
potential and his education and training. If he hadn't been
injured, Reinhard knew he'd been destined to advance rapidly
in the Kriegsmarine, but now he had to take a different
course. He'd heard rumblings among his circle of friends and
military colleagues that Hitler intended to invade the Soviet
Union. Reinhard knew this was a terrible mistake and such a
decision would be the ultimate nail in the coffin of the Third
Reich. Germany could not sustain and could not win a war
against much of Europe and the Soviet Union. It was insanity.
Reinhard was not a Nazi. He despised Hitler as a low-class

charlatan who had seized power illegally and led Germany into an unnecessary war that would ultimately be a disaster.

When Adolph Hitler's armies invaded the Soviet Union and Operation Barbarossa began in June of 1941, Reinhard knew with certainty that Germany would lose the war. It was time to prepare for life after Germany. He began to make plans for his future in the United States of America. His opportunity to realize this dream of living in the USA came with his participation in Operation Drumbeat. Reinhard called in some favors and used his family's contacts to be assigned to a Class IXB U-boat as the chief supply officer. These larger, long-distance submarines led the assault in the waters off the East Coast of the United States and were responsible for the first attacks that marked the beginning of Operation Drumbeat. Reinhard's submarine was scheduled to make several trips to the U.S. Mid-Atlantic Coast during 1942. Reinhard's duties on the U-boat, which made the trip across the Atlantic Ocean from its berth in Lorient on the west coast of occupied France, had been more difficult and painful than Reinhard had imagined they would be. U-boat assignments were for the young and healthy, not for someone with constant pain in his leg.

Reinhard had never married, and his father had died early in World War Two. After grieving for a year as a widow, Reinhard's mother had married a wealthy Hungarian Count and would live the rest of her life in Hungary. Reinhard's two brothers and several cousins were all fighting for Germany in various European countries and on the Russian front. Reinhard wondered if any of them would live through the war. The war had taken his family from him, but he was determined to survive the conflict, even if it meant abandoning his U-boat and forsaking his country.

Once Operation Drumbeat was underway, Reinhard knew that the U-boat's trips to the United States coast gave

him his best chance of coming out of the war with a bright
future, a future he had decided would be spent in the United
States. Reinhard's English was excellent. He had an accent,
but he could work on that once he was living in the land of
the free. Having decided to defect from the U-boat service,
Reinhard made his plans.

Nazi Germany's battle to destroy the United States
Merchant Marine and cripple ocean-going commerce along
the Eastern Seaboard began in January of 1942. What few
Americans remembered from the First World War was that a
German submarine had destroyed ships off Fenwick Island,
Delaware in the waning days of that conflict. As they cruised
off the Delaware coast, the German crew of U-117 had left
deadly mines in the ocean, which exploded and blew a large
hole in the hull of the Minnesota, a 456-foot-long battleship.
The Minnesota was severely damaged, but its crew acted
quickly and brought the ship limping back to Philadelphia.
A civilian cargo ship, the Saetia, also became a victim of
German mines as it sailed off the coast of Fenwick Island
in the late summer of 1918. A devastating explosion ripped
through the vessel, and seawater rushed in as the crew des-
perately launched lifeboats. The Saetia sank, but the crew
was rescued by the United States Coast Guard.

German submarines had shown their capabilities in the
early part of the Twentieth Century to conduct long-range,
trans-Atlantic operations to destroy American civilian
shipping and naval vessels. The strategy had worked well
during World War One, and the Germans immediately set
out on a similar course shortly after hostilities began with
the Americans in World War Two.

Caught off-guard in the Atlantic as well as in the Pacific,
in early 1942 the United States Navy floundered as it tried
to find a way to protect domestic shipping from the U-boat
attacks. In spite of the fact that convoys had been effective in

protecting shipping in the North Atlantic before the United States entered the war, the U.S. Navy was reluctant to use this tactic during the winter and spring of 1942. It seemed as if Navy decision-makers spent all of their time trying to keep secret the truth that hundreds of ships and thousands of sailors' lives were being lost to German submarines. People who lived along the coast knew what was happening, but the Navy was determined to muzzle the press and keep news of the attacks from the public. The full extent of the destruction that resulted from these early U-boat strikes would not become well known until years after the end of the war.

Second only to the shoals off Cape Hatteras, German U-boat commanders preferred the area near Cape Henlopen, Delaware, the area around the 38th parallel, for attacks against Merchant Marine ships. Tankers and freighters heading for the Delaware River congregated around Cape Henlopen and provided a target-rich environment for U-boat assaults. Prowling German submarines could almost always find a mark in these waters.

On January 27, 1942 the German submarine U-130 sank the Francis E. Powell with a torpedo off the coast of Delaware. Seventeen members of the tanker's crew were lucky to be rescued by a passing ship and taken to Lewes. A week later, German submarine U-103 torpedoed and sank four American ships.

The Jacob Jones, a United States Navy destroyer, was sent to patrol the mid-Atlantic coast to protect the shipping lanes. The destroyer cruised without its lights and at a slow speed to avoid detection by the submarines, but on February 28, 1942, it was hit by two German torpedoes that blew a huge hole in the destroyer's hull. Most of the crew were trapped inside and went down with the ship. A few sailors were able to throw life rafts into the ocean and tried to save themselves by escaping over the side of the destroyer. The men who had not been caught inside the ship struggled to climb into the rafts. As the destroyer sank, the depth charges on the Jacob Jones detonated and killed all those who were still aboard. The explosion also killed most of the men who had escaped the ship and were fighting for their lives in the frigid Atlantic waters. Within an hour of the attack, the ship was gone, and most of its two hundred sailors were dead. Only eleven of the crew were saved. The U-boat war against the United States was well underway, and the Germans were winning that war.

– Chapter Six –

Reinhard's Gold

April 1942

R einhard Hoffman, as the chief supply officer of his
U-boat, made all the decisions about what was taken
onto his submarine and where it was stored. Space
was severely limited on a German U-boat, and priority was
given to fuel and to food and water to sustain the crew on
the trip across the Atlantic and back. Fuel was carefully monitored, and every German U-boat that crossed the Atlantic
carried as much as possible. When its prowl off the United
States' eastern seaboard was completed, the U-boat had to
have enough fuel remaining to make the return trip to France.

Torpedoes, which would take out Allied shipping and
military vessels, were given critical space on the U-boat.
Torpedoes were so important and space was so limited that
"the eels," as torpedoes were called, were placed in seamen's
bunk beds at the beginning of a cruise. After a few torpedoes
had been fired, torpedoes were rearranged, and more bunks
became available to the crew for sleeping.

Because Reinhard was in charge of loading supplies onto
the submarine, he could bring whatever he wanted aboard

the U-boat. When his U-boat made its next cruise across the Atlantic Ocean, he planned to carry with him a metal trunk full of gold and American money.

As he poured over maps of the United States and searched for the location of his future home, Reinhard paid particular attention to the Mid-Atlantic's coastal beaches. Reinhard thought the area of the Delaware coast where U-boats liked to hunt had the greatest potential for his personal plans. The area south of Lewes, Delaware was sparsely populated, and the shoreline between Rehoboth Beach and the Indian River Inlet appeared to be very accessible. Significant parts of the coast south of the inlet all the way to the Maryland-Delaware state line were also relatively uninhabited. There were few people to watch for submarines, making it easier to go ashore from the U-boats.

During a previous trip to the Delaware coast, Reinhard had kept his eyes out for a place to bury the fortune that would finance his new life in the United States. He had looked at the terrain on the map and made note of approximate locations and distances. Reinhard needed to find a spot to hide his trunk that would never be discovered, but a spot that he could easily relocate. When he returned on his final voyage, Reinhard planned to slip over the side of the submarine when it surfaced at night. The German deserter would swim to shore and find his way to a new home. When the time was right, he would dig up his chests full of gold and currency. Reinhard would escape into the civilian world of the United States, and no one would ever suspect he had once been a sailor on a German U-boat. First, however, he had to bury his treasure.

He identified a large area just south of the Indian River Inlet that was owned by the state of Delaware and designated as a state preserve. Reinhard guessed this piece of land would always be protected, and no bulldozers would be digging up the sand to build houses or roads. Almost no houses could be found along this particular stretch of coastline. Only one small cottage sat by itself behind the dune; this house would be Reinhard's landmark to remind him where his treasure was buried. Similar wooden-shingle beach houses were scattered along the Delaware coast, but to avoid confusion, Reinhard intended to take a picture of the house near where his trunk was hidden. Then he would know exactly where to dig once he made his final escape from the U-boat and the German Navy.

U-boats stayed hidden under water during the day and surfaced at night when they searched for prey. Resort towns along the East Coast were reluctant to ask residents and summer visitors to turn off their lights after dark. Local authorities did not want to alarm the public with stories of U-boat activity. That would be bad for tourism and bad for business. Consequently, the Germans had an excellent view of what was happening in all of the Delaware beach towns during the summer months. Americans would be shocked if they knew how easily their German enemies could reach the shoreline. There were rumors that daring Germans, who spoke English well enough, donned civilian clothes, came ashore, and mingled with the families who strolled along the boardwalks and bought ice cream as they enjoyed their summer holidays.

Reinhard planned to take a raft onto the beach to hide his treasure chests during his spring and summer forays to hide his treasure. He realized he would have to enlist the support of his submarine commander to successfully carry out these nighttime visits to land. It was, of course, completely out of the question for anyone aboard the U-boat, including the commander, to know the real reason he wanted to take a rubber raft over the side in the middle of the night. Reinhard thought he could make up a logical cover story to persuade his commander. It was essential that the commander of the U-boat believe Reinhard's reasons for wanting to leave the U-boat at night and take the raft to shore. Reinhard would need the help of several members of the crew to get his raft into the Atlantic.

When a U-boat left its birth in France and made an initial mad dash across the Atlantic to cause trouble for the Americans, it carried fresh food for the crew— fruits, vegetables, and meat. As the days went by, the crew consumed the fresh food, then had to eat the loathsome dried and canned provisions. The non-perishable diet available in the waning days of a voyage was depressing for the men who dreaded one more meal of beef jerky and beans. Reinhard knew the area around Cape Henlopen was a rich agricultural area. Sussex County had many farms, and almost every farm and household had its own vegetable garden.

Reinhard proposed to his U-Boat commander that he be allowed to take a raft ashore at night to try to find fresh food for the crew. The commander was skeptical about the risks involved in such an effort, but Reinhard, as supply chief of the U-Boat, was enthusiastic and made a convincing case. His English was excellent, and he felt as if his trip ashore would be successful. The commander reluctantly agreed to Reinhard's plan to take a raft to the beach after the U-Boat surfaced. Reinhard's real plans, of course, were very different than what he'd told his commander. His intentions, once he landed his raft on the Delaware Coast, were much more personal than he wanted anyone to know.

The captain would have to position the U-boat at exactly the right depth in the water to make possible the wet deck launch that Reinhard's rubber raft required. The watchman in the conning tower would have to be made aware of the unusual activity that was to occur the night that Reinhard's raft left the U-boat. Reinhard would use the sturdy oars on the raft to move himself, his trunk, and the treasure in the rucksack back to the shore.

Reinhard took great care with his preparations and paid attention to every detail. He planned to bring his load of gold, currency, and valuables aboard the submarine on each of the next two trips he made to America. He believed in redundancy and would bury two trunks close to each other but not together. The trunks had to be substantial enough to hold his gold bars and coins until he was able to retrieve them. If one trunk were accidentally discovered, Reinhard would have a backup trunk full of booty to finance his dreams. Reinhard knew he would have to be very circumspect as he transferred his valuables and the metal trunk from the submarine to the shore. He would leave some of the treasure in the trunk and carry some of the gold bars and coins in a rucksack on his back. It would be a very heavy load, but the reward would be worth it. Reinhard had a basket specially made in France, which would exactly cover the outside of his metal trunk, making it appear that he was loading a rectangular basket into the raft. The captain and crew would believe the basket was to bring back the foodstuffs Reinhard had promised to find in the Delaware countryside. Only Reinhard would know that a metal trunk rested inside the basket.

Once on land, things would begin to get tough for Reinhard. Already weighed down by the heavy rucksack full of gold on his back, Reinhard would have to move the metal trunk across the sand and dig a hole deep enough to bury his treasure. The execution of the plan would require significant time, strength, and stamina. On the tightly constructed U-boat, small trolleys on wheels were used to move supplies from place to place along the narrow hallways. Two or three of them would be used to move a torpedo into firing position. One of these trolleys, which was about the size of a metal cafeteria tray, would be perfect, Reinhard thought, to move his metal trunk across the sand. Reinhard had fashioned a rope harness to loop across his shoulders and chest to pull the trolley that held the trunk. Reinhard thought he could pull the trunk across the sand to the spot where he chose to dig his hiding place. The trolley and the sturdy shovel he needed would have to be kept hidden from the rest of the crew.

When the time came for Reinhard to make his trip to shore, he maneuvered the raft loaded with treasure into the Atlantic. As he rowed through the surf, he congratulated himself on how easy it had been so far. But when he reached the soft sand, his luck changed. Reinhard had not spent much time on sandy beaches, and he didn't realize how difficult it was to move something across the sand, wheels or no wheels. Germany did not have many sandy beaches. Reinhard had been to the French Riviera on vacations with his family, but most of those Mediterranean beaches consist of pebbles and stones. Reinhard did not realize how difficult it would be to move the trunk until he had lifted it from its custom-made basket onto the trolley, put the rope harness around his chest and shoulders, and pulled. Nothing happened. The wheels of the trolley dug into the sand and wouldn't move. Although Reinhard's upper body strength was significant, his injuries had left him with a weak leg, and he struggled. Finally he ditched of the trolley, tied the heavy rope around the trunk, and hauled the trunk along the sand. It was tough going, but at least the trunk was finally moving. Reinhard fought for each few inches, but eventually he was able to drag the trunk away from the surf and closer to the dunes.

Reinhard knew the farther from the high tide mark he buried his treasure, the safer it would be. Reinhard had read that in this area tidal surges accompanied hurricanes and northeastern storms, and he wanted to bury his trunks far enough from the ocean that even a very bad storm would not disturb them. The reality of moving the trunk a great distance beyond the dunes made him rethink his options. As he panted and pulled his load forward, he wondered just how far from the water he absolutely had to be before he could start to dig.

When he finally chose a spot, he was exhausted. He unloaded the heavy backpack and sighed with relief. Now he had to begin to dig a very deep hole wide enough to contain the trunk. The deeper he dug the hole, the safer the trunk would be. Once again, his plan was challenged by the difficulty of digging a hole in the sand. The sand kept falling back into the hole, and the sides of the hole kept collapsing. Digging a hole in the sand was not like digging a hole in regular dirt, and the more Reinhard dug, the more sand fell back into the pit. He realized he should have brought some kind of a bucket to help him carry the sand away from the dig. Pre-school children who had spent summers digging in the sand at the beach could have educated Reinhard on the necessity of bringing one's pail if one wished to dig a hole of any functional worth. Without a pail, Reinhard felt as if he had been shoveling for hours without much to show for it, but having come this far, he continued his labors. He would have preferred to dig deeper but compromised on a less than perfect hole for the trunk.

He transferred the contents of his rucksack to the trunk, lowered the trunk into the hole, and began to fill the hole with sand. He hoped no really bad storms would tear up the beach before he was able to get back to recover the treasure. Reinhard thought it would only be a few weeks or months until he returned to dig up his secret in the sand. He was counting on good luck to guarantee that no ambitious tourist or child would start to dig and by accident discover what he had buried.

The location Reinhard had chosen was within sight of the cottage near the dunes. He could not risk burying his trunks on the land owned by the State of Delaware. That would be asking for trouble. He had been lucky enough to acquire a land use map that showed what land was government-owned and what was private property. Reinhard was very exacting about where he'd bury the gold and currency that would finance his future. The dunes within sight of the gray shingle cottage were the perfect site.

When Reinhard finished covering up his trunk, it was three o'clock in the morning. He was completely worn out and soaked in his own sweat. He still had to try to find fresh food to take back to the U-boat. If he brought back something good from this trip ashore, his commander would be more willing to allow him to take a raft to the beach the next time they were off the Delaware Coast. Reinhard was spent, and his leg was causing him a lot of pain. But he felt as if he had to find something worthwhile to take back to the U-boat.

He had heard a rumor among the crew that there was a small store on the paved highway, and he'd found the store marked on a map of the area. It didn't sound like it had much to offer in the way of fresh fruits and vegetables, but Reinhard was going to give the place a chance. It would take him almost an hour to walk to the store and almost an hour to walk back. He hid his raft and took off across the dunes. When he reached the main road, he was alone as he walked in the direction of the store. Not a single car passed him this early in the morning.

When he finally reached the little store, he found a shack that looked even less promising than it had sounded. Reinhard easily broke into Nate's Baits and General. He found potatoes, apples, beets, and a few onions in crates on the floor and a few heads of lettuce, two heads of cabbage, and a dozen or so pears on shelves, along with what looked like bread products. Reinhard filled the two burlap bags he'd brought with him. He took as much food as his bags would hold and he could carry. He topped the booty off with several bottles of bourbon. The two heavy bags were awkward and slowed him down on his return trip to the raft. He was in a lot of pain as he dragged the bags behind him, and he was afraid the sun would come up before he was able to return to the U-boat.

He finally made it back to the raft, which he pulled down to the shoreline. He quickly loaded his burlap bags bulging with groceries into the now empty basket. The sun would be peeking over the horizon any minute, and he was ready to push off into the ocean. After burying his treasure, then walking for more than two hours to find the food, he was desperate for a drink of water. When he saw that the nearby cottage had an outside pump on the porch, he scarcely fought the temptation to risk getting a drink. Water was rationed on the U-boat, and he could almost taste the heavenly liquid from the pump flowing down his throat. Even though something warned him that this was not a good idea, he ran to the house. The pump mechanism began to squeak and moan as he worked the handle. He wondered if anybody were at home or if anyone were trying to sleep. Surely they must be able to hear that someone was using their pump.

Elizabeth was sound asleep in her canopy bed, her dogs snuggled at her feet. Since April was sometimes cold at the beach and it could even snow in Delaware in April, her windows were tightly closed. Still the sound of a squeaky pump was easily heard inside the house. All of a sudden, Licorice and Vanilla raised their heads. Both came to attention, and their ears were on alert. Their sudden movements woke Elizabeth from her sound sleep. The dogs began to growl, which they rarely did.

Once a raccoon had been caught in Elizabeth's garden fence. It had screeched and cried, and the dogs had started to bark. Although, Elizabeth didn't like to let them outside

without a leash, they'd made a terrible racket. Elizabeth finally
opened the door, and away they went. Fortunately, the dogs
had not gone near the raccoon but had kept their distance,
barking like crazy. The raccoon finally freed itself and ran
away into the night. Another time a skunk had sprayed
its scent outside Elizabeth's window. That got everybody's
attention, and it was days before the smell disappeared. The
dogs also barked like crazy that night to warn her that the
offending skunk was close to the house. Growling was a sign
of trouble Elizabeth hadn't heard from the dogs before. This
was danger of a different kind.

When she heard the squeak of the pump, she knew
something was wrong. Elizabeth had running water in her
cottage, and the pump was left over from a by-gone era. It
still worked, and she used it to water her garden. Somebody
was on her porch and was helping himself to her water. At
first she thought it might be an early morning fisherman
casting for bluefish. Elizabeth knew several of these fishermen
and had told them they were welcome to get a drink of water
from her pump when they were thirsty. But the dogs knew
the fishermen were welcome at Elizabeth's house and didn't
become alarmed when they came onto the porch. Because
April was really too early for Elizabeth's fisherman friends
to be going out for bluefish, she knew something wasn't right
on this dark morning.

Elizabeth kept a shotgun loaded with birdshot in her
pantry. The shotgun was there to scare away the deer and
other critters, which came to feast on her garden. The garden
was fenced in, but occasionally a deer made it over the fence
or a groundhog made it under the fence. This early in the
season only a few perennial herbs could be seen above
ground, and the dogs were not warning her about critters
this morning. Elizabeth put on her warm, woolen dressing
gown and retrieved the shotgun. If she fired it at a person or

a critter from a distance, she wouldn't seriously harm them. This was not a gun that was intended to kill animals or people, just to warn away an unwanted intruder, whether it was the two-legged or four-legged variety.

Elizabeth walked outside and around to where the pump was located. A scruffy looking man with a beard stood next to the pump guzzling water. He was not a fisherman or anybody she recognized. This was a man she had never seen before. Elizabeth approached the man from behind, raised the shotgun, and demanded to know what he was doing on her porch.

The startled man turned around. Water dripped from his chin, and his eyes grew wide as he stared at the shotgun. He had not expected to be confronted by a white-haired woman holding a firearm. He jumped over the porch railing and took off running across the dunes. Elizabeth shouted for the man to stop, but he kept moving. She noticed he ran with a distinctive limp, but he was still able to move very quickly down the beach. She fired the shotgun into the air to scare the man. She didn't want a person she didn't know coming to her porch and using her pump in the middle of the night. If he had introduced himself, asked her permission, and been polite and respectful about it, she would have been happy to allow him to get a drink.

The sun had not yet started to paint the sky with slivers of dawn. Elizabeth might have run after the intruder if she'd been dressed and had her flashlight with her. At the sound of the shotgun, the dogs had gone crazy until Elizabeth let them out of the house. She left the shotgun on the porch and made her way over the dune to the water's edge. Dressed in her full-length navy blue robe, she was quite a sight as she walked through the sand.

She looked down the beach in the direction the man had taken. Licorice and Vanilla were at her heels. Elizabeth heard what sounded like a raft or small boat being launched into the surf, and then she heard oars dipping into the water. At this hour of the morning, the man on her porch had to be the same man who was rowing quickly out to sea. Elizabeth listened and peered into the early morning fog until the sound of the oars died away.

– Chapter Seven –

Smile!

April 1942

E lizabeth walked down the beach to the place where she thought the man had made his escape into the surf. In the half-dark, half-light of the early morning, she discovered a curious contraption. A small trolley on wheels had been left at the water's edge. If the tide had been coming in rather than going out, the strange device would have been swept into the ocean instead of remaining like a small whale beached on the sand. Elizabeth examined it. Who brings a trolley with wheels to the beach? It was a very odd thing to do. Elizabeth decided to make a more thorough search of the area later in the day. Maybe she would find more clues to help solve the mystery of what idiot would try to use wheels in the sand. Elizabeth dragged the trolley to her house. She decided to go back to bed and try to get a few more hours of sleep before investigating further.

That afternoon, Elizabeth explored every inch of her dune. She found a large shovel and some ropes tied together to make a kind of harness. The rope was not the kind found on a sailboat or attached to an anchor line. This rope, made of thick, sturdy hemp, was the sort one found on a farm.

The objects Elizabeth had collected did not help her solve the mystery, but she was sure something nefarious had been going on near her home the night before. She needed to show what she had found to someone in law enforcement. Somebody needed to hear about her early morning visitor. With all the explosions occurring off the coast, one always had to wonder about German U-boats and the possibility that enemy agents might be coming ashore. Elizabeth was a very rational person and did not immediately think of treachery, but these strange artifacts, each by itself and the three in combination, were certainly intriguing.

Elizabeth carried the shovel and the rope back to her house. She arranged the three clues on a bed sheet and snapped photographs of them from all angles. She knew she would never see the actual trolley, rope, or shovel again, once she had turned her evidence over to law enforcement, so she wanted to document what she had found. She'd been a decent amateur photographer when she lived in Washington. D.C., where she'd been lucky enough to have her own dark room. She'd taken lots of photos of her children and her gardens and developed all of her own pictures. When she'd made the decision to move to Bethany Beach, she knew there would be no space for a darkroom, but she'd brought her camera with her. There was so much beauty to be captured close to the ocean, and she loved taking photos. She mailed her rolls of undeveloped film to Kodak, and they sent back prints. Elizabeth took close-up shots of a manufacturing stamp on the steel blade of the shovel and of the writing in gothic German script she found on the underside of the trolley. She was curious about the unusual foreign markings.

Elizabeth loaded the items into the back of her truck and drove to Georgetown, Delaware. Her encounter with the sheriff's office earlier that year had not gone well, but she thought if she presented him with actual physical evidence rather than just her anecdotal account about ships burning off shore, he might pay more attention to what she had to say. She honestly did not think she would do any better with the sheriff this time than she had the last time, but she didn't know where else to turn.

With a war just getting underway, men of all ages were leaving their civilian jobs to join the military. Every region of the country and almost every business were experiencing employment shortages. As might be expected, many law enforcement personnel were leaving their positions to fight our enemies abroad. Elizabeth was certain the sheriff of Sussex County would say he did not have the man-power to investigate the story of her intruder. No one had been injured. Nothing had been stolen. Just the opposite, in fact: the intruder had left the tools of his trade behind.

The sheriff surprised her with the interest he showed in Elizabeth's discovery. He had her repeat twice what she had seen and heard. He took notes about what she said to him and carefully examined the shovel and the trolley. After taking Elizabeth's name, address, and phone number, he told her someone from the Coast Guard might come by to talk to her. She told him she was happy to do whatever she could to help. Finally, somebody was paying attention to what she had to say. She was glad she had made the trip to Georgetown. As she drove back to Rose Cottage, she felt as if a burden had been lifted from her shoulders. She hoped no more unwelcome visitors would trespass on her property tonight or any other night.

Because she'd found a shovel, Elizabeth hypothesized that someone had been digging on the beach. She didn't know whether they'd been digging a hole to bury something or digging up something. After she returned home from her

trip to Georgetown, Elizabeth explored every inch of the
dune around her house and didn't find anything that looked
suspicious. Nothing looked like it had been recently dug up
or buried. The bearded man who had been digging had done
a good job of covering his tracks. Because he had made such
a quick escape by sea, he could not have been carrying much
of anything with him. She couldn't help but wonder if the
nighttime caller had been burying a body in her dunes.

Elizabeth's first instinct was to want more lights installed
outside her house, but she immediately rejected the idea. Even
though the additional lighting would have made Elizabeth
feel more secure, she decided to sacrifice personal security
for national security. During wartime, especially along the
coast, lights left on at night could attract attention from the
enemy. She still did not understand why the authorities had
not asked beach residents to turn out their lights at night and
use blackout curtains after dark. She was not in charge of
making decisions for anyone but herself, but common sense
told her that if the country was at war, it needed to act like
it was at war.

Reinhard made it back to the U-boat just before it submerged. Reinhard hadn't counted on the physical exertion
the job had required, nor the time it had taken, and he'd not
counted on someone shooting at him with a shotgun. He was
exhausted after his night on the beach and decided to think
things over after he'd slept, when his brain was refreshed and
working better. As he'd madly rowed back to the U-boat in
his raft, he remembered that he had left the trolley and his
shovel behind on the beach. He had intended to stow all of
his gear back in the raft after he'd buried the trunk, not leave
it strewn all over the sand for the old woman or someone
else to find.

Reinhard was thankful he'd taken the time to walk to
the bait and grocery store and steal the little bit of food

and drink he'd been able to find for the crew. The men were not especially thrilled about the onions and the beets, but Reinhard scored points for the white bread, the pears, and especially for the bourbon. He felt sure his commander would allow him to take the raft ashore again during their next visit to the area. His commander liked American bourbon.

If Reinhard had known that the house near where he had chosen to bury his treasure was inhabited by a crazy woman with a gun, he might have tried to find a different location. It was too late to worry about this, especially since one of his very valuable trunks was now buried on the woman's property. It would be foolhardy and way too much work to dig up the trunk and bury it someplace else. That was not going to happen. He had another trunk to bury and would be better prepared when he went ashore the next time. He definitely would not be bringing a trolley with him on his second trip to the beach, and he definitely would be bringing a pail to help him dig the hole. He would be much more discreet and careful in the future. Reinhard had learned some lessons.

One thing he had to consider was whether he should try to photograph the shingle house on the beach, the cottage where the old woman with the shotgun lived. He wanted pictures of the house to document exactly where he was burying his financial future. Many small houses in the area were built out of gray shingles, and they all looked alike to Reinhard. He wanted pictures so he would remember the environs, even weeks or months from now, and be able to identify the exact house near where he had hidden his gold. He did not want to spend his time digging in the dunes around the wrong house.

He had to take the photographs of the woman's house during daylight hours, and that almost made Reinhard abandon his plan. He would have to leave his U-boat at night to come ashore, and then he would have to hide himself and his raft until daylight. After he'd taken his photos of the house, he'd have to conceal himself for the rest of the day while he waited for nightfall. Only then could he safely return to the U-boat.

Reinhard's U-boat was scheduled to return to France in three days, which meant that he would need to return to the beach tonight if he were going to take his photos during this trip to America. He did not want to go ashore again so soon after his recent encounter. The more he thought about it, the more it seemed like taking the pictures was going to be more trouble than it was worth. He couldn't make the trip to shore without the help of the crew getting the raft on and off the submarine. He couldn't have the help of the crew without the knowledge and permission of his commander. Disappointed, he acknowledged to himself that he wouldn't be able to take the photographs during this trip. He didn't want to forget where he had buried all his gold, but now the only choice was to remember the location of the house. He'd try to find it again on his next trip to the U.S.

After a few hours of sleep, Reinhard was able to resume his duties as supply officer for the rest of the day. He was in the mess talking to his fellow sailors about his adventure of the night before when he'd taken food from the American grocery store. Reinhard was just about to return to his bunk for the night when the submarine's commander came into the mess and asked to see Reinhard in his quarters. Sweat broke out on Reinhard's forehead, and his heart raced. Had the commander discovered what Reinhard had really been doing when he'd gone ashore? How could he? No one but Reinhard knew anything.

Reinhard stood at attention while his commander explained that he'd been on the radio with the German High Command. He had told them the story of Reinhard's successful foray to the Delaware coast. They had been amazed by Reinhard's bravery and ingenuity. One of Germany's military goals had been to put someone ashore from a U-boat to do reconnaissance of the coast during daylight hours. There were things German generals and admirals were anxious to know about fortifications along the Mid-Atlantic beaches. They were hungry for first-hand information and had very specific questions they wanted answered.

His commander had been ordered to ask Reinhard if he would go ashore again to do some spying during the day. Was Reinhard willing to take the risks involved in making a second trip to land? Germany would be very grateful, and Reinhard could count on receiving a promotion and perhaps an iron cross if he would agree to the dangerous mission.

Reinhard could scarcely contain his amazement. He had given up on the idea that he would be able to go shore to take photographs of the location where he had buried his treasure. Now his commander was begging him to go ashore during the daylight hours. Reinhard couldn't believe his good luck, but he didn't want to appear too eager. He asked his commander what kind of reconnaissance he would be expected to undertake. He asked if he was qualified to do that kind of work. His commander was supportive and encouraging.

Then the commander brought an old-fashioned 35 mm camera out of a cupboard in his quarters. He asked Reinhard if he'd ever used a camera like it. Reinhard had used a 35 mm camera before the war and was happy to tell his superior officer that he was very familiar with the Leica. Reinhard wanted to pinch himself. Not only was the commander of his U-boat begging him to go ashore for reconnaissance, but now he was asking Reinhard to take photographs of what he saw. It was Reinhard's lucky day. He graciously agreed to take the assignment, although he knew he didn't really have a choice. The commander feigned delight and told Reinhard he would have orders for him at 0400 hours the next morning. He told Reinhard to get some sleep and report back for special duty at that time. Reinhard was to wear civilian clothes on his mission, and these would be provided to him.

When Reinhard reported to his commander's quarters the next morning, the commander gave him the civilian clothes and two pages of questions the German High Command was interested in having answered about fortifications along the Delaware beaches. The clothes didn't really fit at all, and Reinhard felt silly in the pants that were too short and too tight.

The Coast Guard Station between Bethany Beach and Dewey Beach and several of the watch towers which had been constructed along the Delaware coast, were of special interest to strategists in the German military hierarchy. Reinhard was to find out the size of each facility, how many personnel were assigned to each one, what material the towers were made of and how far each of them was from the road and from the high tide water mark. There were several other questions that required taking measurements.

Reinhard had been instructed to shoot as many photographs of the facilities as he could, without attracting attention to himself. It was a big assignment, but Reinhard was more than happy to undertake it especially since he'd be able to take photographs of the house where his gold was buried. Reinhard packed the commander's 35 mm Leica and extra film in his duffle. What the commander didn't know was that Reinhard had already secreted another camera in his bag. Reinhard had an expensive German subminiature Minox camera, a tiny thing that took pretty good pictures. The camera was made in Latvia by a German manufacturer, and the film was very expensive. Reinhard would have to be discreet when he was back in France and took the film to be developed.

Reinhard's entire plan, from burying the trunks full of treasure to his defection from the Kriegsmarine when the time came, had to be accomplished in total secrecy. No one could know he intended to leave his German U-boat and military command, his German family and heritage, and in fact his entire German identity and life behind to begin a new life in America. If his plans were discovered, he would be branded a traitor.

Reinhard's raft left the U-boat just before dawn when his submarine submerged for the day. When he arrived on the beach for the second time in two days, he was able to bury his raft under the sand among the scrubby beach vegetation. There were no people on the beach, and he remained out of sight until it was light. He headed toward the house where he had run into so much trouble two nights earlier. Staying close to the water, he adjusted the Minox and began to shoot his photos. It was so early in the morning, he thought he could accomplish this mission without anybody noticing him.

He was so intent on accomplishing his task, he failed to see that the woman, whose house he was photographing from the shore line with his tiny camera, was also photographing him. Elizabeth was standing on her front porch. She had the telephoto lens on her camera and was taking close-up pictures of Reinhard's face while he was taking pictures of her house.

She didn't know with absolute certainty that this was the same man who had been using her pump two nights earlier, but she was pretty sure he was. She'd had a quick look at the man on her porch, and even though it had been dark, she thought this man had the same build and the same coloring as her middle-of-the-night visitor. The beards were exactly the same. Why would this man be photographing her cottage this morning? Why was such a person showing so much interest in her, and why was he hanging around? Elizabeth was not a woman who was easily frightened, but seeing this bearded man near her house twice in two days put her on alert.

Reinhard focused his Minox on the details of Elizabeth's house, the gardens, and the surrounding dunes, never noticing that she was on her porch with her camera taking pictures of him. As soon as he had taken all the photos he needed, he walked back down the beach. Elizabeth called her dogs and tried to follow the man, but she lost him. She noted that the man with the camera had a serious limp. Because the man who had been using her pump had also walked with a limp, Elizabeth was convinced this was the same man. She had to admit he was good at disappearing.

Reinhard stowed the Minox in his duffle and set out to accomplish the tasks his commander had assigned to him. For most of the day, he walked up and down Route 1, trying to be inconspicuous as he photographed everything he thought might be of strategic importance to his commander. He measured, counted, estimated, and might have even fabricated here and there, when he couldn't get the exact answers that had been requested.

Reinhard was growing tired when he approached the last watch tower on his list. He began to measure its distance from the road. A man walking his dog along the highway approached Reinhard and asked what he was doing. The man grilled Reinhard about his camera and about the measurements he was taking. He wanted to know why Reinhard wasn't in uniform. Reinhard was hesitant to speak because he was afraid his English would sound foreign to real Americans. But he improvised and exaggerated his limp when he told the man he was in the civil service and doing work on the towers and the roads. The man wanted to see his ID, but Reinhard refused to show the man anything. The man with the dog had not shown him any official badge or paperwork, so Reinhard ignored him. The man threatened to call the authorities when he got home. It was time for Reinhard to complete his mission and lay low.

Reinhard made his way back to where his raft was hidden and dug a hole in the sand to hide himself until it was dark. After a couple of hours, he had sand stuck to his skin and in every pocket and wrinkle of his clothes. He was hot. He had brought food and water with him this time, but it was full of sand and almost inedible by the time he got around to eating and drinking. It seemed like nightfall took forever to arrive. Finally, it was dark enough for Reinhard to emerge from his hole in the sand, uncover his raft, and row his way back to the submarine.

Reinhard's commander welcomed him as if he were a conquering hero when he returned to the U-boat that night. Reinhard turned over the information he had collected during his day ashore and returned the commander's camera and the several rolls of film he'd shot. He told his commander he was tired and needed to go to his bunk. The U-boat commander could not do enough for Reinhard, who hoped nobody would require the services of the chief supply officer that night, at least until after he could get some sleep.

Reinhard's plan, which had seemed so straightforward when it had been an idea in his mind, had become a great deal more complicated in the reality of its execution. Reinhard had learned a number of things the hard way. At age twenty-five and given his war injuries, he realized the complicated and strenuous operation to bury his treasure was almost beyond his strength and abilities. He had another trunk to deliver to the United States and bury in the sand. He was glad he would have several weeks to rest before he had to undertake the next phase of his project. Maybe the old harridan in the gray shingle cottage would die before he made his next U-boat journey west across the Atlantic Ocean. One could always hope.

– Chapter Eight –

The Wise Man Arrives

Last July

Lane and Louisa avoided mentioning the subject of treasure to each other for a whole day. They were excited and frightened by their discovery, and they dreaded telling their parents about it. Finally, the girls gathered their courage and tried to figure out how to bring up the subject with the adults. Their very intelligent cousin, Austin, who was nine, was arriving the day after tomorrow. The girls decided they would put off saying anything to anybody about the treasure until they'd had a chance to talk things over with Austin.

Austin would know what to do. He had known the capitals of all the states in the United States when he was three. He knew all about DNA and the Revolutionary War. He could play the guitar really well and had started his own kids' rock band. He would be able to talk to the adults, tell them what the girls had discovered, and ask for suggestions about what action should be taken. They were relieved after making their decision to wait for Austin's wise counsel before doing anything further.

When Austin and his mother arrived from California for the July Fourth week, he had an agenda of his own. He wanted to attend as many baseball games as he could with his cousin Tyler. They shared a passion for the sport, and Austin wanted to watch his gifted older cousin play in tournament games. This family vacation, spent at their grandparents' beach house in Sandpiper Dunes on the Delaware coast, was the only week during the year when the five cousins were able to be together. The other thing on Austin's list was to organize the family talent show. Many were reluctant to perform, but Austin was the master of ceremonies and inspired his family members to participate. He was not prepared to hear the unbelievable story his girl cousins told him the afternoon he arrived at the beach house.

At first he thought they'd made up the tall tale or that their story was part of an elaborate game they had invented for fun. When Lane and Louisa took him to the bunk room and pulled the plastic container out from under Louisa's bed, his eyes nearly popped out of his head. He could see that their wild account about finding treasure hidden in the sand was for real. Perhaps for the first time in his life, Austin was speechless. He was so stunned by what he had heard and seen, he just didn't have anything to say. He had to think things over. A wise man always thinks before he speaks.

When he finally found his voice, he told them they had to talk to the grown-ups about their discovery. Neither Lane nor Louisa had been brave enough to look in the leather pouch for the gun, but Austin said that if there really were a gun in there, it was dangerous to have it lying around the bunk room. It was without question a very old gun, since everything else in the trunk was very old, and sometimes old guns malfunctioned or went off by accident when they weren't supposed to. Austin was more concerned about the safety of the gun than he was about the gold and currency the girls had found. He proposed they call a meeting that everybody in the family would be required to attend. The meeting would be held after dinner that night.

After the dinner dishes had been done, everyone gathered as directed on the screened porch of the beach house. The adults were anxious because they didn't know what the agenda was for the family meeting. They called most family meetings and they knew the agenda ahead of time. This family meeting had been called by their children, who had not shared with anybody what they would be discussing. The adults now understood what it was like to worry about an unknown agenda.

Austin, using the skills he displayed as master of ceremonies for the family talent show, opened the meeting. He was solemn and looked each of the four parents and two grandparents directly in the eyes. "Lane and Louisa made a remarkable and incredibly exciting discovery on the beach two days ago. Because the tide was coming in and threatened to swamp the treasure they had found, they decided to bring it to the bunk room to protect it. I think everyone will agree, once they have heard the entire story, this was a wise decision on their part. I am going to turn the floor over to Lane to tell her story about how she and Louisa found gold in the sand."

When Austin mentioned gold, a couple of the grown-ups gasped. Grandpa Bob laughed. He didn't believe anybody had found real gold on his beach. He sniffed and said, "Humph, Fool's Gold, maybe."

Lane ignored his comment and proceeded to tell the story of how she and Louisa had found their amazing prize. Louisa interrupted Lane multiple times because she wanted to be certain that every detail was told exactly as it had really happened. Louisa was especially insistent that everyone know she had discovered the first gold coin, the clue that treasure was buried in the sand. Lane had brought one of the gold coins with her to show to the parents and grandparents. She handed it to her father, who turned it over and over in his hands. He had a very, very serious expression on his face when he handed the coin to Lane's mother for her to examine. The adults passed the coin around the room from one to the other. Not one of them was an expert on coins or even had a coin collection. Nobody knew what they were holding, but it definitely looked old. And it looked valuable.

Lane went on to explain how much gold had been in the trunk they'd found, how they had carried it all to the bunk room, and where it was now. She added at the end of her narrative that she thought there might be a gun in one of the disintegrating leather pouches she had deposited in the container under Louisa's bed. The parents were stunned. They were as speechless as Austin had been when he'd heard their story.

The parents realized this was not a time for scolding or talking about taking responsibility. The kids had behaved responsibly under the circumstances, and they had realized it was important to inform their parents and share their excitement and their fears. Even though the girls had struggled with how to divulge the information, this was not a matter of failing to disclose anything or attempting to hide the truth. This was not about being naughty or trying to circumvent the rules.

Abbey, Louisa and Tyler's mother, was the first to recover her ability to speak. "I think you girls should be congratulated on the way you have handled your discovery. You thought things through and behaved in an organized and sensible way. You did what you could do by yourselves, and when you realized you could no longer handle things without help, you called us in to give some advice—with Austin calling all the stakeholders together for the meeting. I think you've done everything you should have done, and I'm proud of you."

Chris was glad that somebody had begun the discussion and echoed Abbey's positive spin. "We'll have to have a look at your treasure, and we might even need to call in some experts to accurately evaluate what you've found. Why don't we go down to the bunk room right now and take a look at what you have? We can go from there."

Everyone who hadn't seen "the treasure" was dying to get a look at what all the fuss was about. Perhaps it would turn out to be something left over from a treasure hunt of years gone by. Maps handed out for a birthday party game might have been intended to lead children to a treasure chest full of pretend money, and maybe the chest had never been found until now? Or maybe, somebody's camp trunk or a seaman's trunk was lost at sea and finally had washed ashore after years of ocean storms and floating on the waves. None of those scenarios, however, could explain the gold ingots and the coins.

Gram opted not to go down to the bunkroom. She didn't do very well with stairs, and everyone had to go down quite a few steps to see the treasure waiting under Louisa's bed. Chris and Grandpa Bob led the way. Grandpa Bob was the only person in the house who knew anything at all about firearms. He was a quail hunter who hunted with a shotgun. Old, rusty handguns were not really in his purview. Louisa insisted on pulling the plastic bin out from under her bed. Tyler and Robbie wanted to be in the front row to see what was happening. Their noses were out of joint because they'd been left out of the excitement their sisters had created.

When Chris lifted the lid of the plastic container, he actually gasped out loud. He knew before he touched the first coin that it was the real thing. These were not tokens from the Jolly Roger or fake money left over from a long ago birthday party treasure hunt. The gold ingots were real. Chris looked at the bundles of thousand dollar bills wrapped in crumbling, yellowed cellophane packets tied up with deteriorating leather ties. He picked up one of the bundles and checked the date printed on one of the bills. It was United States currency, for sure. He realized with a start that he was holding a fistful of thousand dollar bills. The date on the bills was 1928.

The first thing everyone wanted to take care of was the gun. Chris asked Lane to point to but not touch the leather pouch that held the offending weapon. She knew exactly which one it was. She had put it in the plastic container. Chris handed the leather pouch to Grandpa Bob and asked him to take it outside and lock it in his truck. They would examine the gun later. Right now, everybody wanted it out of the bunk room and out of the house. Grandpa Bob took the gun to his truck. He looked at the gun briefly and decided it was a German Luger, a semiautomatic pistol popular with the German military during World War II. He locked the gun in the glove compartment. He would take it to the bank as soon as possible and put it in a safety deposit box. The Luger would be safe at the bank until Bob could take it to a gun dealer. If the gun were an old German model, it might be the first evidence that the trunk had been buried by someone who had a connection to Germany.

Every one of the adults was pretty much speechless when they saw the treasure in all of its reality. Looks went back and forth among the grown-ups as if they were wondering who was going to take charge of this problem and what in the world they were going to do about it. Tyler and Robbie wanted to touch everything and hold the coins and the ingots of gold. Chris cautioned them about keeping their hands away from the contents of the container.

"This might be stolen from someplace, and we don't want to get any of our fingerprints on it. We don't know that any crime has been committed, but just in case, let's try not to contaminate a possible scene with our own fingerprints.

I know I already touched some of the things in there, and I probably shouldn't have."

Abbey and Gretchen were both lawyers, but their legal specialties did not include the kind of law that could shed light on who legitimately owned a treasure found buried in the sand. Neither one had ever before needed to know anything about the laws governing buried treasure. Gretchen did know that these laws differed from state to state. In some states, found treasures belonged to whoever discovered it. It was finder's keepers. In other states, the treasure belonged to whoever owned the property on which the treasure was discovered. In still a third category, the treasure belonged to the state government in whichever state it was found. Gretchen thought California might be one of the states in the third category. She didn't know what the law was in Delaware, but she intended to find out the answer to that question tonight.

Because the girls had found the treasure so close to the water's edge, it could be argued that it had been either found at sea or found on the land, depending on the location of the high tide water mark. Maritime law was murky about the ownership of centuries-old ships and their contents discovered at the bottom of the ocean. The ownership of the treasure found on sunken Spanish galleons, which had carried gold from the New World back to Europe in the days when the United States was a British colony, was a case in point. To whom did that long-lost treasure belong?

Abbey had noticed some old-fashioned gothic script used in pre-World War II Germany on some of the papers in the plastic container and suspected they were looking at Nazi riches. Because of the existence of the Luger, the parents were guessing that the treasure had once been owned by someone with a connection to the Third Reich. The Third Reich no longer existed. The treasure sitting on the floor of the bunk room probably could be traced to someone who had lived in a country whose government had been out of business for more than seventy years.

Gretchen realized that when caches of valuables were discovered, people lined up to claim ownership. Charlatans were known to steal from the innocent and naïve people who had made the discovery. Gretchen was intent on protecting her loved ones from those who might try to lay claim to the treasure the girls had found. Possession was nine points of the law. Proving the treasure belonged to somebody else would be difficult. This family had the treasure and nobody else had it. Who had a better claim to it than they did? But things could get complicated.

Gretchen knew there would be a long and arduous process involved in trying to figure out who ultimately owned and could legitimately claim the treasure. The immediate issue was what to do to secure the valuables, to keep them safe tonight. It was eight o'clock on Friday evening, and this was all happening at a beach house just before the July Fourth holiday weekend. There wasn't any wall safe behind a painting available to them. All the banks were closed, and they couldn't store any of the booty in safety deposit boxes for three days. They had to figure out what to do with the treasure for the night and for the long weekend.

Lane and Louisa were tremendously relieved they had finally shared the burden of their discovery with their parents. It helped to have the grown-ups giving them advice about something so momentous. Louisa, whether she wanted to admit it or not, was thankful to have someone take responsibility for the gun that had been under her bed for several nights. The presence of the gun had not kept Louisa awake, but she was really, really glad it was gone now.

The lines in Lane's forehead had disappeared. Her knowledge of the treasure and the fact that her parents had known nothing about it had weighed heavily on Lane's very responsible shoulders. She felt physically and mentally lighter, but she noticed that the lines in her mother's forehead had deepened after she'd found out about the treasure. Lane felt bad about this, but she knew the information about their discovery and the responsibility for doing something about it had to be transferred to the adults.

– Chapter Nine –

Old Money

Last July

Before the kids went to bed, they helped sort the treasure into categories and put it into more manageable containers. Chris had insisted whoever touched anything at all had to wear protective gloves. Gram had plastic containers of all sizes and shapes, and each category of the treasure went into a separate container. The gold coins all went into one container. The small gold ingots went into another container. The "greenbacks" went into another. The containers were stored under Chris and Gretchen's bed.

There had been a collection of papers, passports, and photo IDs in the bottom of the trunk. Lane and Louisa had felt it was important to try to save the papers as well as the obvious valuables. Everybody assumed the papers were written in German. Gram and Bob had once upon a time been able to read German. Almost nobody except German people knew how to read German these days. Gram took the papers to her room to try to figure out what they said.

When the plastic container was almost empty, Lane found several small velvet bags at the bottom. These bags, nearly overlooked in the rush to save the treasure from the rising tide, had been thrown into the container in the bunk room with everything else. Lane overheard her mother and father talking about the content of the velvet bags. Her parents tried to keep their voices low, but Lane thought she'd heard the word diamonds mentioned more than once. Gram told her family she would take charge of the velvet bags. She would put them in her safe deposit box at a local bank as soon as the bank opened.

After the treasure had been sorted, counted, inventoried, and hidden again at the beach house and the exhausted children had gone to sleep, the adults sat around the antique pine dining table. They were anxious to talk about how to deal with this shocking and unexpected development in their lives. They all wanted to believe the treasure was real. A variety of specialists would ultimately have to be consulted to prove the provenance and authenticity of the valuable artifacts, but the parents, eager to find out what they could right now, stayed up late into the night doing internet searches. It was a good thing to have smart parents, and these parents would figure it out. Some parents would just have called the police or the FBI and turned it all over to the government. These smart parents wanted to have as much information as possible before they called in the authorities who would no doubt want to confiscate everything and keep it. That was not going to happen in this case.

Austin's mother Joanie had a background in business and finance and was curious about the current value of the treasure. The ingots felt like real gold. Markings on the gold bars indicated that each one weighed a kilogram, which equaled one thousand grams. This made each gold bar worth whatever a kilogram of gold was selling for that day.

None of the parents knew anything about pre-World War Two European money or antique coins. The coins the girls had found were mostly Swiss, Austrian, and Danish, and many years had passed since the coins had been put in the trunk and buried in the sand. Gold always held its value, and some of the coins might be worth a great deal more than their face values. Joanie got busy on the internet and found hundreds of pictures of gold coins listed on various websites and on eBay. Some of the coins she found on the internet looked similar to the ones in their treasure trove. She was shocked to find that one rare antique coin could have a face value of twenty Swiss francs but in fact be worth many thousands of dollars. Antique coins could have added value because they were collectors' items and worth a great deal to coin collectors. These numismatists were willing to pay considerable money for special coins. Experts in Washington D.C. would need to be consulted about the coins and gold bars.

The paper currency was United States issue and appeared to be the real thing, but it would have to be examined by an expert to verify that it wasn't counterfeit. Joanie researched the 1928 issue currency and found that even though it was decades old, it was still negotiable. The money in the packages looked as if it had never been circulated. The bills were crisp and, in spite of their age, felt brand new. Thousand dollar bills were very rare and hardly ever seen outside a bank vault even in the present day. People did not carry around thousand dollar bills in their wallets and purses. How could a store make change for a purchase if someone paid with a thousand dollar bill? These days, most places wouldn't even take a fifty dollar bill because they were afraid the bill might be counterfeit.

Chris had once seen a thousand dollar bill with Grover Cleveland's picture on it, but none of the other adults had ever seen one. Imagine how unusual it would be to have had stacks and stacks of thousand dollar bills before or during World War Two. How in the world had anybody ever put his or her hands on so much American money? Whoever had accumulated this vast wealth must have had connections with a bank that had access to international currencies. They all wondered if the money been stolen from a bank.

Chris had estimated, just based on the face value of the bills, that there was more than a million dollars' worth of thousand dollar bills in one plastic container. Joanie had discovered during her internet research that if the money were real, special mint marks, letters, or stars could make individual bills worth considerably more than a thousand dollars because they were valuable to collectors. It was impossible for Chris to hide the anxiety he felt about having all this cash stored under his bed.

How odd that the person who had buried all these riches must have been, at least from the evidence they'd been able to discover so far, a German and probably a Nazi. What was he doing with all this United States currency? What was the money doing buried in the sand of the Delaware Beach? That mystery was one they might never unravel.

The immediate question, and the question that would be the most difficult to answer, was who owned the treasure the two girls had found. Special lawyers would have to be consulted. There was a consensus around the table that the United States federal government would try to confiscate the treasure and keep it. Grandpa Bob was adamant that "his girls" had found the cash, the gold, and the gems, and it all belonged to them. He was not going to allow the government to take anything else from him or anybody he loved.

Lane and Louisa had told their parents about the rusted pieces of the trunk they'd rescued from the tide and reburied next to the dune fence. It was a dark night, and the moon was new. The family sensibly had decided to delay until morning the recovery of the remains of the rusty trunk. The girls would go down to the beach with Lane's dad as soon as they awoke. There was probably nothing useful to be learned by salvaging the lid and the broken pieces of the trunk, yet it was something that had to be done.

The next morning the girls went down to the beach with Lane's father and Grandpa Bob. They took a cardboard box to bring the pieces of the trunk back to the house. They didn't have to dig very deep to find the rusted out remnants and the lid. The girls had buried it just a few days earlier, and they'd been in a hurry. They carried this last part of their treasure back to the house. Nobody thought these rusty pieces of metal would be of much importance—at least compared to the gold coins and the other obvious valuables. But having the pieces of the trunk in which the treasure had been hidden all these decades might be necessary to prove the age of the treasure and document its origins. The lettering on the trunk was indeed the gothic script used in Germany before and during World War Two. The pieces of the trunk, which had almost been carried away with the tide, might be definitive proof of who had buried the treasure.

Gram was the keeper of the diamonds and there were hundreds of them. Some of the diamonds in the velvet bags were quite large. None of the parents knew much about gemstones or their value, but it seemed as if there was a considerable fortune in diamonds now resting on Gram's bedside table. The diamonds would have to be examined by a jeweler to determine if they were real.

Gram had a long-time friend whose nephew was a jeweler in Baltimore. Gram called her friend and made an appointment to meet with the nephew. Gram didn't want to meet at a jewelry store or at a commercial diamond exchange, so they agreed to meet at her friend's home. After the July Fourth family vacation, Gram would drive to Baltimore with the diamonds to get an expert's estimate about what the diamonds might be worth.

If indeed the diamonds were genuine and worth a significant amount of money, Gram already knew she wanted the proceeds from the sale of the diamonds to go towards setting up an educational trust fund for her grandchildren. She might decide to keep a few of the stones to have made into earrings for her daughters or engagement rings for her grandchildren for the distant future, but she wanted to cash in the diamonds for a portfolio of blue chip stocks that would grow and yield enough interest to finance her grandchildren's educations. She wanted them to be able to afford to attend the best schools they could get into.

Each of her three daughters had gone to excellent secondary schools and colleges. Tuitions to these schools had been steep in the 1990s, but the expense of private secondary education and college was becoming costly beyond the means of ordinary people. Lane and Robbie attended a very good private school in Washington D.C., and Austin attended a school for gifted children in Palo Alto, California. Abbey's kids went to public school, and she would love to be able to send them to private school. Abbey wanted her kids to be in classrooms with fewer children than the public school was able to provide.

Gram knew education was a top priority for all the parents, and help with private school tuitions would be welcomed. Nobody in the family was anxious to spend their good fortune on fancy yachts, fur coats, or frivolous luxuries, and everybody already had a nice house. Education was the cornerstone of everything this family stood for, and Gram wanted to help her kids and grandkids by setting up a trust to pay for good secondary schools, colleges, and graduate schools. It was her dream. The diamonds would make her dream a reality.

Gram knew something about tax law and knew that if the money from selling the diamonds were used to fund an education trust, no income taxes would have to be paid on it. The trust would need to be set up very carefully by a financial advisor and an attorney who specialized in this type of law. If it all were done the way it was supposed to be done, some of the treasure from the sand could be set aside to educate the children in the family for generations to come.

Everyone was excited that this serendipitous largess might be coming to them, but the adults were worried that word would leak out about the discovery of the treasure. The press loved a story like this. The parents realized they needed to shield themselves and their children from the media hoopla that would inevitably surround such a find. Thieves loved to find a family that wasn't sophisticated about guarding tangible riches. Keeping the discovery of their treasure a secret was paramount. Having such a financial windfall was mind-boggling to this family that had never dreamed of having anything they had not earned themselves through hard work.

The parents knew how important it was not to talk about what was going on, but nobody had seriously discussed with the children the importance of keeping the news of their discovery private for the time being. Lane and Louisa had kept their secret very well for several days and knew they had to continue to maintain silence. Austin and Tyler were both old enough that they understood the gravity of the situation, and who would they tell anyway? The wild card in the group was Robbie. He was six, and no one had bothered to sit down with him and tell him how important it was that he not say anything to anybody about the discovery of the treasure.

– Chapter Ten –

The Summer of '42

July 1942

The Americans finally figured out that the German Navy had arrived at their shores. Asleep at the wheel for too many months, someone in the United States Navy noticed that our Merchant Marine fleet was being decimated within sight of the homeland. Hundreds of U.S. ships had been torpedoed, and thousands of lives had been lost. It was as if surprise and then denial had paralyzed the United States military into inaction. This failure to respond was not characteristic of Americans, and once they finally got their act together, the sleeping giant was roused.

Convoys were organized to protect the merchant ships. Military vessels, already in very short supply, were requisitioned to guard the convoys as they traveled along the coast. Powerful guns were installed on Liberty Ships, and special crews on loan from the Navy were assigned to sail on Merchant Marine ships to man the guns. Factories were finally ramping up the production of ships to protect the convoys.

Reinhard realized that the free reign to destroy, which the U-boats had enjoyed along the Atlantic seaboard in the early days of the war, would not last much longer. The Americans were finally reacting, and The Second Happy Time was coming to an end. Reinhard had yet to bury his second trunk full of treasure in the sands of the Delaware beach. He had learned some lessons from his first experience a few months earlier and would do better with his second effort.

No one in his family had discovered anything about the liquidation of the family assets in Dusseldorf; so no one had questioned his purchase of millions of dollars worth of diamonds from the proceeds of the liquidations. No one realized that Reinhard had appropriated holdings from his family's bank and requisitioned the packets of thousand dollar bills in American money. He had covered his tracks with clever bookkeeping and would be long gone before anyone at the bank traced the disappearance of the money back to him.

Reinhard had stolen the gold bars outright from the vaults at the bank. These were held as reserves, and bank employees didn't pay much attention to them. They'd been in the bank's basement for decades, and Reinhard didn't think anybody would take the time and trouble, especially with a war going on all round them, to count the bank's gold bars and notice that some were missing.

Reinhard figured the bank itself might be long gone by the time anybody began to look for the greenbacks and the gold he had taken home and buried in his garden. The bank might physically disappear in the rubble of an Allied bombing raid. Or the bank might disappear as an organizational entity when the Allies marched into Germany and put out of business anything and everything that had been remotely associated with the Nazis. This was what the Nazis did when they conquered a country, and Reinhard figured the Allies would do the same to German institutions. He felt he was covered except for the coins.

Some of the gold coins had belonged to Reinhard's grandfather's coin collection. Before he died, his grandfather had spent countless hours researching and studying his coins. All during his childhood, Reinhard had heard family members say that his grandfather's coins were very valuable. When the war started, the collection had been transferred for safekeeping to the family bank. Reinhard had appropriated the entire collection for his buried treasure, and he had exchanged more of the bank's gold ingots for additional gold coins.

Reinhard thought he would be able to use the gold coins and the currency to finance the initial phase of his life in America. He knew he would have to include smaller denominations of American money to buy things at stores, but he had the idea that some of his gold coins would be legal tender in the United States like they were in Europe. Swiss twenty franc gold pieces were welcomed at any and all places of business in the Third Reich and throughout the continent, and Reinhard thought the Swiss money would be welcomed everywhere in the United States as well.

Reinhard wanted to buy a small farm in Delaware, where he could begin his new life. He had a forged American passport and other false identification papers. He had a phony birth certificate and phony papers from the United States Navy granting him an honorable discharge because of his injuries. He really did have war-related injuries, and he really did have a limp. Of course, his story was a lie because when he had acquired his wounds in the war, he had been fighting for the Germans, not for the Americans. Any man within a certain age range who was not in uniform or doing some kind of government service during the war was immediately suspect in Germany. Neighbors and friends as well as the authorities all wanted to know why such a young man was not fighting for his country, why he had civilian status.

Reinhard assumed this would also be true in the United States. Every able-bodied man had either volunteered or was being drafted to join the Army or the Navy or the Coast Guard. It was mandatory. For a man in his twenties or thirties to show up and not be wearing a uniform would arouse suspicion. Reinhard would need his counterfeit discharge papers and his limp—as well as his stash of money—to be accepted as a disabled war veteran and farmer in a small town on the Eastern shore of the Chesapeake Bay, also known as the Delmarva Peninsula.

Reinhard had poured over maps of Delaware while planning his life as a farmer. Because he would not be able to farm the land himself, he'd have to hire workers to till and harvest the fields for him. He would, of course, buy a farm with a house on it. Reinhard had been studying the small towns in the area and decided he liked the town of Roxana, Delaware as a place to look for his farm. Money would be no object, but he would have to make his real estate purchase carefully and discreetly.

Reinhard would find that, for many reasons, buying the farm he wanted would prove to be more difficult than he anticipated. Because of the war, every acre of farmland was dedicated to growing crops and raising livestock. Every spot of ground not being used for these purposes was planted in "victory gardens." Many people had plans to dig up their entire backyards and plant vegetables that they could harvest and preserve. Food rationing would come soon enough, and anything Americans could grow themselves became important. It was not going to be easy for Reinhard to find a farm to buy. Farmland was like gold everywhere during wartime.

Reinhard had hired a lawyer from Liechtenstein, who was working on acquiring the farm for him. He'd learned from his lawyers that purchasing property in another country, especially in a country with which one's own country is at war, presents another set of problems. Since the war had started, Americans had become increasingly suspicious about all kinds of transactions with people from overseas. Reinhard would find that buying property through a foreign lawyer raised suspicions in this provincial part of the country. He would be buying his farm under an American name; he had a birth certificate, a passport, and other paperwork in that American name. Even when one had the funds and the proper papers, purchasing a farm was turning out to be difficult.

Reinhard did not want to give anybody in the German military or anybody else he knew the slightest hint that he was trying to buy real estate in America. The purchase had to remain a total secret, and Reinhard's new American identity also had to remain secret. Reinhard, through his lawyers, was trying to finalize a real estate transaction that required signatures and official paperwork. The process was proving to be challenging and time-consuming.

Reinhard's lawyers in Liechtenstein had briefly considered using members of the German American Bund in the United States to expedite the purchase of the Delaware farm. The German American Bund was an organization of American citizens of German descent. Their main goal was to promote a favorable view of Nazi Germany in the United States. Since the beginning of the war, this group had been very closely monitored by U.S. authorities. The Bund was not a very smart bunch of fellows. They were rabble-rousers and liked to draw attention to themselves. That kind of help Reinhard didn't need. The idea of enlisting the help of the German Bund was dropped because it could too easily become counterproductive.

Instead, the Liechtenstein lawyers hired lawyers in the United States to help with the purchase of Reinhard's farm. They advised Reinhard it was going to take some time to finalize the purchase and suggested he find temporary living quarters in America while negotiations for the farm were underway. Real estate deals could fall through for various reasons. There were many variables to be considered. The purchase of the farm would go more smoothly if Reinhard were already living in the United States and could go to settlement and sign the paperwork for the transaction in person. He instructed his lawyers to find him an appropriate place to stay once he'd left his U-boat for the last time. With the mobilization for war, all housing was at a premium. Rentals and places in rooming houses were scarce.

Planning his new life was getting more and more complicated for Reinhard. Communications between Reinhard and his lawyers were difficult. He could easily make contact with them when he was in France, but when he was aboard his submarine in the middle of the Atlantic Ocean, he was almost incommunicado. But Reinhard was clever. Because he was a supply officer and had some access to the ship's radio, he had worked out a code with his lawyers so he could send and receive messages to and from them while he was at sea.

Small towns in the United States were often very insular communities, especially before World War Two. Many farms were handed down in families from one generation to another. These family farms rarely came on the market for the public to buy. People in agricultural areas were sometimes suspicious of outsiders, and country people in the United States could be closed-minded. Purchases of property through holding companies and absentee landlords was routine in Europe, but this type of impersonal transaction was not as commonplace in rural America. In Delaware, a man who sold his farm wanted to know the person who was going to buy it. Navigating the idiosyncrasies of the provincial Roxana, Delaware real estate market added another level of difficulty to Reinhard's farm purchase.

The farm in Roxana was the perfect size for Reinhard's needs, and it had the perfect house on it. Reinhard had his heart set on the place that he had only seen in photographs and on drawings of the site. The owner was ambivalent about selling his farm, and when he finally agreed to sign a contract, he stipulated that he wanted to delay the settlement. Because the farm had been in his family for many years, he was having a difficult time letting go, and although he needed the money, he also needed time to come to terms with his decision to sell. Reinhard offered, through his lawyers, to increase the amount he was willing to pay for the property if the seller would agree to an earlier settlement date. Even the offer of more money was not enough to entice the farmer to sell more quickly.

Reinhard's lawyers were working to find temporary lodgings for him in a rooming house. His other option was to begin the entire search all over again for a different farm. Reinhard didn't want to do that. He wanted the farm in Roxana. He decided he was willing to live in a rooming house temporarily and wait as long as he had to wait to take ownership of the farm he had his heart set on.

Reinhard was frustrated. He had assumed that if he had enough money, he could have whatever he wanted—even in the United States. That was the way it had been in Europe. All one had to do was grease a few palms with sufficient cash, and you could have anything. That European model wasn't working in America. Reinhard had wanted his farm to be signed, sealed, delivered, and waiting for him when he made his last trip to the Delaware coast. He wanted a seamless transition from U-boat to Delaware farm. He felt this would minimize any chances that his true identity and background as a former German military man would be exposed. Now his timetable was ruined, and even with trunks full of gold and cash, Reinhard couldn't have his way.

Reinhard had made a very careful and detailed plan, and he believed he'd thought through every contingency that might prevent his plan from working. As soon as his second trunk of gold and currency was buried, he would be ready to abandon his U-boat and begin his life as an American. He had been practicing his English and thought he was making progress speaking without an accent. Reinhard would test the truth of that assumption when he finally walked into a small town in Delaware and began conversing with the locals.

Reinhard worried briefly that the old woman who had shot at him might recognize him if he lived anywhere close to her cottage. He might run into her in the post office or the hardware store. Reinhard was going to shave his facial hair before he left the U-boat for the last time. Without his dark beard and mustache, no one would be able to recognize him as the former submarine supply officer. When he left the German Navy, he would shed the looks and the persona of a German U-boat sailor and begin a new life.

Hiding the second trunk went much more smoothly than had the burial of the first one. The moon was out the night Reinhard left the U-boat to bury his second cache of valuables, so he could see where he was going and what he was doing. Reinhard brought his own water this time and stayed away from the cottage with a pump on the porch. He had brought a bucket as well as a shovel to dig his hole. He had a better harness to pull his trunk behind him in the sand. He was able to dig a deeper hole, and burying the second trunk required less time and effort. Reinhard was more efficient and didn't encounter any people during his shore excursion.

After he had put the last shovel full of sand on top of the second trunk, he almost decided to wing it. He was tempted to walk into one of the Delaware towns he had been fantasizing about and try to get a room at a boarding house on his own. But confidence in his ability to pass himself off as an American had not quite reached the point where he was willing to risk such a step. He was afraid he might have to go from rooming house to rooming house to find a place. The idea was tempting to Reinhard, but because of the challenges such a spontaneous course of action might present, he decided he was not yet ready to take the chance.

After a good bit of self-deliberation, Reinhard chose to stick with the plan his lawyers had laid out, to wait until he had living quarters guaranteed in his new American identity. The less he had to interact with Americans when he first left the U-Boat, the better it would be. Once he had practiced his English and had gained more self-confidence about speaking with the natives, the more secure he would feel about moving freely among them and pretending to be a Yank.

Reinhard had originally hoped he would be able to leave his German life behind immediately after burying this second trunk. He was disappointed about the delay in the purchase of the farm but decided he would wait to abandon his U-boat until it made its next trip to America. He would have to wait to become a Delaware farmer.

He had plenty of time to revisit Nate's Baits and General and procure food for the U-boat crew and several bottles of bourbon for his commander. Reinhard was back on the U-boat in a few hours and was pleased he had accomplished his mission. He had photographs of the cottage, which marked the spot where he'd buried the trunks. He knew exactly where to dig to retrieve his fortune when he returned. He was ready.

But there would be no next trip to the coast of America for Reinhard Hoffmann. He would never recover the vast treasure he had secured for himself in the sands of the Delaware beach. He would never buy the farm in Roxana. He would never shave his beard, and he would never have to worry about running into the old lady with the shotgun at the grocery store or the post office.

Reinhard's U-boat had just started east on its return trip to occupied France. It was cruising on the surface of the Atlantic Ocean, thinking it was home free. Every other trip to and from the coast of the United State had been uneventful, and the U-boat had always arrived and departed completely unchallenged. This trip ended very differently. Lulled into complacency that the Americans would never achieve success in defending their shores, Reinhard's commander and crew were taken by surprise when the attack came. An armed Coast Guard patrol boat was cruising the waters off the coast of Long Beach Island, New Jersey near Barnegat Light when it fired on and sank Reinhard's U-boat. The guns, which had just been installed on the deck of the Coast Guard boat, fired at the U-boat's aft fuel tanks where all of its remaining fuel was stored. When the fuel storage area was hit, the submarine exploded. The U-boat broke in half, then sank. No members of the crew were rescued when all hands went down.

Reinhard's dreams would never be realized. His time and his luck had run out. He was now just another casualty of war among tens of thousands. Less than two days after he had buried the second part of his fortune, he perished in the sea. Reinhard's gold and treasure, his secret in the sand, would stay buried north of Bethany Beach, Delaware, undiscovered for almost seventy-five years.

– Chapter Eleven –

I've Got Plenty of Nothin'

Last July

Robbie was six years old. The gold coins were shiny, exotic, and enticing. It wasn't fair that the girls had been the ones to discover the treasure, and now they were getting all the attention. Robbie wanted to have one of the gold coins to touch and hold in his hand. He wanted to keep one as a souvenir. He thought of all the ice cream and Legos he might be able to buy with one of them, if they were worth as much as everybody said they were. Nobody was going to miss one coin. There were so many in the plastic container under his parents' bed. There were hundreds and hundreds. Surely, he could take one. He put his purloined coin under his pillow for safekeeping. He would have to think about what he was going to do with his piece of the treasure.

Robbie kept the coin under his pillow the entire week of the July Fourth vacation. He decided he would take it home with him to Washington D.C., so he hid it in his backpack. Maybe in the fall when he entered the first grade, he would take the coin to school for Show and Tell. He was sure it would make a big hit when he handed it around to his classmates, especially when he told the story about how his sister and cousin had found treasure in the sand. That would be the most exciting story any first grader could hope to share with the class. He was sure nobody had ever seen anything quite like his coin, and nobody had ever heard a story quite like the one he had to tell. He would love to have taken one of the gold bars, too, but the parents had counted all of those and made a list of how many gold bars they'd transferred to the bank. They would have noticed if one of the gold bars had gone missing.

When their vacation week came to an end, Austin returned to California with his mother. Lane and Louisa would leave soon for sleepover camp in Lewes, Delaware. Their camp was a music camp, and they would spend three days learning and singing songs of all kinds. Abbey and Gretchen had signed Tyler and Robbie up for a boogie board day camp in Bethany Beach. It was going to be so much fun. Robbie was just old enough to qualify, and he was excited to be doing something with the older boys.

On the first day of camp, Robbie took his special coin with him in the pocket of his bathing suit. Kids of all ages had come to the camp to improve their boogie boarding skills, and Robbie was not the smallest, even if he was the youngest. One other boy was smaller than he was. There were lots of big boys. Some of them were really big. Several scary boys looked like they spent a lot of time working out. Their hair was spiky, and they had real tattoos on their arms and backs and on their legs. Robbie had put tattoos on himself numerous times, but they were the kind you could wash off or the ones that disappeared after a few days. These big boys looked like their tattoos would be on their bodies until they died. The boys with the tattoos talked very rough, too. They said words that Robbie's mom and dad had told him he was never to say. Robbie was afraid of these tattoo boys. They were not like anybody he had ever been around before. He wondered why they were here in Bethany Beach pretending to learn how to boogie board. It was obvious to Robbie they already knew how to use a boogie board and were very good at it.

After lunch on the second day of camp, Robbie was sitting on a bench by himself. He was turning his precious gold coin over and over in his fingers. Two of the tattoo boys sat down on either side of him. Robbie was nervous and wanted to leave and sit someplace else. One of the tattoo boys grabbed the gold coin out of Robbie's hands and looked at it closely.

"Where did you get this money, pipsqueak?" the bully demanded.

Robbie was tall for his age and knew he was not a pipsqueak. It made him angry that these bullies had taken his coin and were calling him names, but he was too afraid to say anything.

"I think I'm going to pinch this coin and buy myself something really nice with it. A little boy like you wouldn't know what to do with gold." The bullies were taunting him.

Robbie just wanted to get away from the two bad boys who were being mean. He didn't even care if they took his gold coin. Finally, he found the courage to speak. "You can have it. I don't care what you do with it. I have lots more where that came from. Just get away from me." He stood up and tried to walk away, but the two toughs moved to either side of him and blocked his way. Robbie felt threatened.

"What's your name, little boy, and where do you live?" said the bully with the most tattoos. "You say you have lots more where this one came from? Where are those lots more where this one came from, huh, huh?"

Robbie had a feeling he should never have said he had lots more where that coin had come from. Just then, an air horn alerted the boys that the afternoon session was about to begin. The bullies were momentarily distracted by the sound, and Robbie was able to run back to where the instructor was standing near the water. Robbie was nervous for the rest of the afternoon. The big boy bullies kept looking at him, and one of them made a gun with his thumb and forefinger and shot it at Robbie. Robbie felt sick to his stomach by the end of the day.

What no one noticed when Tyler's mother picked up the two boys in Bethany Beach that afternoon, was the old jalopy with Pennsylvania license plates that pulled out behind Tyler's mom and followed her car home on Route #1. When Abbey turned into Sandpiper Dunes and parked in front of their beach house, neither she nor the boys paid any attention to the old jeep with a torn canvas top that slowed down near the driveway. The boys in the disreputable vehicle watched Abbey, Robbie, and Tyler get out of the car and climb the stairs.

Robbie said he was sick and didn't want any dinner. He didn't want to think about going back to boogie board camp the following day. That night he couldn't fall asleep. He had lost his gold coin, but he told himself he didn't really care about that. No one had known he'd taken one in the first place, so no one would ever know he'd been too afraid to get it back from the bully boys. He would not have the coin to show when he started first grade, but he could still tell the story. The gold coin would have made his tale of buried treasure so much more believable.

Tyler and Robbie were sleeping alone in the bunk room. In the middle of the night, the sound of breaking glass made Robbie sit up in his bed. He looked at the bunk room door that opened on to the outside deck and noticed that a pane was broken. Shards of glass lay all over the floor. Robbie's heart turned over when he saw the two boys who had been mean to him in Bethany Beach that day. They were standing in the doorway of the bunk room. How had they found him? One of them made the gun with his thumb and forefinger and again pointed and shot it at Robbie. At first Robbie thought he was having a nightmare, but he quickly realized this was real, that the bullies had come to his house to get him. He wanted to scream, but he was so frightened, he couldn't make a sound. One of the bullies grabbed a blanket from the bed and put it over Robbie's head. He could scarcely breathe and begged the boys not to hurt him.

"Shut up, pipsqueak! Don't you dare scream or cry or call for help. All we want to know is where you've hidden the coins. You said you had more where that one came from, and we want to know where they are."

Robbie's response was muffled as he tried to explain to the boys that the treasure was no longer here at the beach house. It had been taken to the bank and put in safe deposit boxes. It was clear the two did not believe him. They told him they would smother him if he didn't tell them where they could find the gold coins. Robbie was sure they would smother him and think nothing of it. He was telling them the truth when he said the coins were no longer in the house, but the bullies wouldn't listen. He didn't know what to do. He felt helpless. He was afraid he was going to die.

Then the bullies told him they were going to take him with them. They were going to kidnap him and hold him for ransom. They said they would write a note to Robbie's parents and demand the rest of the gold coins in return for not harming Robbie. They would return Robbie to his parents only when they received the rest of the gold coins. Robbie was certain the bullies meant what they said. He began to wish they would just smother him.

What the bully boys did not know was that Tyler was in the bunk above Robbie's. He was a very sound sleeper. Tyler's mother always said it took an earthquake and a brass band to wake him in the morning. The commotion and the bullies' loud voices had awakened Tyler. He'd heard the bullies threaten Robbie. He'd heard them say they would smother him. He'd heard them say they would kidnap him and hold him for ransom. Tyler didn't know how the bullies had learned about the treasure of gold coins, but he knew he had to do something to save his cousin.

Tyler saw a suitcase lying on the top bunk bed next to his. He knew he could easily reach it from where he was. He could drop it on the head of one of the intruders, but he didn't know how he would incapacitate the second bad guy. Tyler knew he had to do something quickly before they took Robbie away. Then he saw his grandmother's blue and white cane leaning against the door between the hall and the bunk room. Gram had several canes that she left around the house in places where she thought she might need one. She always left one in her car and always left one in the front hall to help her get down and back up the outside steps. If he could just reach the cane by the door, he would have a second weapon and might be able to do something to the second intruder.

Tyler was small for his age but he was very athletic and strong. He was also brave. He was not afraid of anything. Tonight he had a plan to save his cousin. He knew he had to take action as soon as possible but was smart enough to wait for just the right moment. He concentrated on what he was going to do.

He carefully and silently crawled across the bunk beds until he could just reach his grandmother's cane in the hallway. He pulled the cane up onto his bunk. Then he lifted the empty suitcase over his head. He mentally collected his strength and courage. Then, with all his might, he threw the suitcase down onto the bad bully boy who had covered Robbie's head with the blanket. The bully stumbled backwards and lost his footing. He had not been expecting an attack from above. Robbie threw the blanket off his head and joined in the fight. He picked up the suitcase and banged the bully boy over the head with it a second time. He grabbed the offending blanket and threw it over the head of the bully who had been smothering him. Then he sat down on top of the bad guy. There was a small wooden antique chest of drawers beside one of the bunk beds. Robbie had no trouble pulling this chest over on top of the robber he and Tyler had bonked with the suitcase. One burglar was on the floor with a blanket on top of him. On top of the blanket was a fairly heavy chest of drawers, and on top of the chest of drawers sat Robbie. This bully was not going to get away.

Meanwhile, Tyler had jumped off the top bunk with the cane in his hand and began beating the second intruder over the head with it. Once the second bully realized his partner in crime was down, bully number two tried to run. Before he could reach the bunk room door, Tyler reached out, hooked the bully's ankle with the cane, and brought him down. As he fell to the floor, the bully hit his head on the side of one of the heavy wooden bunk beds, and blood began to gush. Tyler didn't really want to kill even this very bad guy, and for a moment he was afraid he had. Tyler was relieved to see that this second burglar was still breathing and had only been knocked unconscious by his collision with the wooden bunk bed.

Tyler was sitting on top of the second burglar when his mother and Robbie's parents burst into the room. Who could sleep through the crashing suitcase, the yelling and screaming, and the colliding of a body against the bed? Of course, the noise had awakened them. Abbey had her cell phone in her hand and was already calling 911. When Grandpa Bob came down from his bedroom, he immediately saw what was going on and went to the laundry room for some clothes line he knew was in a drawer. Clothesline would make an excellent rope for tying up these bad people who had broken into his house and tried to hurt his grandsons. Both of the intruders were trussed up like turkeys when the Sussex County Sheriff's Department arrived.

Law enforcement took the two tattooed criminals away in a squad car. The sheriff interviewed everybody who had been in the house when the attempted robbery and kidnapping had occurred. Tyler told the sheriff's deputy in great detail how the bullies had threatened to harm and kidnap Robbie. The people from the Sheriff's Department were at the beach house for hours. When everybody had told their stories several times, the sheriff told the family the bunkroom was a crime scene and would be off limits until the criminalists from Georgetown could come to gather evidence the next morning. The excitement was over for the night. The exhausted boys fell asleep in another guest room, and everybody finally went back to bed. They all slept very late the next morning. It had been a night to remember.

The CSIs appeared the next morning and spent hours in the bunkroom. They tested all the surfaces for fingerprints. They took pictures of the bunk beds and the splotches of blood where the one bully had fallen and hit his head. They took pictures of the chest of drawers.

The sheriff took Gram's cane as evidence. It was one of her much-loved ones because it was blue and white, Gram's favorite colors. Gram gave the deputy a hard look when he told her he was taking her cane with him. She told him she wanted it back, and he promised her he would be sure it was returned to her. The sheriff also took the suitcase as evidence. Everyone who looked at the suitcase was very impressed that Tyler had been able to knock the intruder over with it. Tyler tried to act as if throwing suitcases was something he did every day, but secretly he was quite pleased with himself. Who knows what might have happened if Tyler had not been resourceful and put his plan into immediate action? He had saved the day, and he may have saved his cousin's life.

Robbie cried and cried as he told his parents about the coin he'd taken from under Louisa's bed the week before and how he'd foolishly told the tattooed boys there were lots more coins where that one had come from. The sheriff said he thought the bullies had followed Robbie home from boogie board camp in Bethany Beach. Nobody was angry with Robbie. Everybody was just happy that Robbie was all right. More than anything, Robbie was angry with himself.

In the end, both Tyler and Robbie were heroes. Together they had foiled the bad guys. There would be lots more interviews, a court case, and a great deal of official "to do" surrounding the nighttime intrusion at the beach house in Sandpiper Dunes. But everybody was safe, and the bad guys would go to jail.

The last thing Robbie wanted to do was to go back to boogie board camp the next day, but Tyler talked him into returning. For the rest of the week, there were no more boys with tattoos and spiky hair at the camp, and the clunker jeep with the Pennsylvania license plates was never seen again in the parking lot. They were safe from trouble for a while.

When the investigation into the attempted robbery and kidnapping in Sandpiper Dunes was completed, there were wide-ranging ramifications that revealed something even more sinister than a break-in at Robbie's beach house. The two culprits that Tyler and Robbie had foiled had long rap sheets. They were not the sixteen-year-olds they claimed to be and had no business whatsoever participating in a boogie board camp for teenagers.

There were four tattooed bad boys, all hardened criminals in their twenties. They were vicious Philadelphia gang members who had targeted Bethany Beach and other Delaware beach towns. They thought rich people kept jewelry and other valuables in their beach houses. The people who owned beach houses in the area might have silver and jewelry hidden some place, but most of them did not bring these possessions to their summer houses. The gangsters from Philly were not only bad, they were not very smart.

When the Sussex County Sheriff's Department realized they weren't dealing with teenage bully boys, but in fact were dealing with criminal adults, they widened their investigation. The four-member gang had broken into a vacant house in Dewey Beach and were squatting there for the summer. That empty house was also where the criminals stored the loot from the various robberies they had committed along the beach from Lewes, Delaware to Ocean City, Maryland.

Law enforcement found tens of thousands of dollars of stolen goods at the house in Dewey Beach. They also found garbage, decayed food, and other smelly and nasty things inside the home. Trash was everywhere, but it could not hide the computers, the iPads, the Xboxes, the surfboards, the radios, the watches, and water skis that the hoods had stolen. There were even three boats hidden in the garage. These goons might not have found the silver and the diamonds they'd been stupid enough to think they could steal from summer vacationers, but they had found enough electronics, sports equipment, and other goodies to make their summer worthwhile. Unfortunately, all of that delicious loot they had gone to so much trouble to steal was now going to be evidence in their criminal trials.

The thieves had signed up for the boogie board camp to have something to do during the days and as a way to meet kids who might talk about their family's valuables. They'd picked up information from other summer camps they'd attended in Delaware's beach communities. The robberies took place at night, and the gang did its trolling for prey during the days. It was particularly infuriating that they befriended and threatened kids for information.

Because Tyler was able to give sworn testimony that one of these crooks had threatened to kidnap Robbie, the accused would probably go to federal prison for a long time. The others would also have the book thrown at them. They might have gotten off with lesser sentences if they'd had a Philadelphia jury, but in Sussex County, Delaware, people were all about law and order, and these guys were toast.

The question that parents and members of the community had was why any of the directors of the summer camps for kids had allowed these creeps, who obviously did not look like the other teenagers, join and participate in activities with younger kids who really were just kids. One coach explained that he'd been very suspicious about why these tattooed thugs had made applications to attend his soccer camp. But they had filled out the required forms and paid their money. They had lied about their ages and presented fake birth certificates as proof of their youth. What could he do? In this era of extreme political correctness, one could be sued or threatened with prosecution if one discriminated against somebody because of tattoos or spiky hair, oversized muscles, or looking old for their age. The coaches had not wanted to accept the sleazy-looking applicants into their sports camps but felt they didn't have a choice.

Tyler and Robbie received a special commendation for capturing these criminals. The cousins pretended it was nothing, that they caught bad guys every day of the week, but they were both thrilled they'd been able to overcome and hold these hardened criminals by themselves. If they'd known how dangerous the men really were, they might not have been so brave. It was an example for all that brains definitely could prevail over brawn—even brawn enhanced by steroids.

Robbie was vindicated, and the gold coin that had caused so much trouble was returned to him by the authorities.

If Robbie had not flashed his coin around at boogie board camp and tempted the gangsters to break into the beach house, the criminals might never have been brought to justice. Gram's blue and white cane was returned to her, and she put it back in the exact same spot in the hall where it had been when Tyler had grabbed it to beat one of the intruders over the head, hook his ankle, and cause him to fall into the bunk bed. You never knew when a blue and white cane might come in handy.

– Chapter Twelve –
Time Changes Everything

1962-2008

Elizabeth was seventy-six years old when the Ash Wednesday Storm of 1962 swept Rose Cottage into the sea. The grey shingled house surrounded by *rosa rugosa* was no more. Elizabeth had left her home near Bethany Beach two years earlier and was living with one of her daughters in the Washington, D.C. area. Arthritis had taken its toll on Elizabeth's joints, and living in a house built on pilings was no longer an option for her. One of her grandchildren drove her down to the Eastern Shore each summer so she could visit Rose Cottage for a few days. She struggled to walk up the narrow wooden steps, and going back down to the car was almost impossible. She couldn't manage walking across the dunes to visit the beach. She missed watching the waves from her screened-in porch and being at the cottage where she'd spent so many happy years of her life. Her beloved dogs, Licorice and Vanilla, were long gone. She had bought a Westie puppy after the pair had died, and that puppy was now ten years old. Time had sailed away.

From the day she had said goodbye to her fancy Washington, D.C. life, all through the terrible World War years, and continuing up until the day she left Rose Cottage, Elizabeth had lived life on her own terms. She would not have changed anything that had been within her power to change. She had accepted the difficulties and occasional indignities of old age with the philosophical attitude that had always been her salvation, her way of coping. Saying goodbye to Rose Cottage had been heart-wrenching for her, but the reality of her infirmities forced her to be sensible and make the decision to leave her house in Bethany in order to live a more a circumscribed existence in someone else's home. Giving up her fierce independence was anathema to Elizabeth. As much as she hated to have to do it, she finally was able to accept that she needed the help of others. Elizabeth took comfort in the fact that, even though she no longer lived there, Rose Cottage endured.

The March 1962 Northeastern storm destroyed many homes and communities on the Delmarva Peninsula. Rose Cottage was one of hundreds that did not survive the tidal surges and the flooding. Elizabeth had taken the furniture and mementoes that were valuable to her when she'd moved to her daughter's house, but when she heard the news that her cottage by the sea was gone, she wept. She grieved the loss of her beloved home, Rose Cottage, and she thought back on the wonderful life she had made for herself there and lived so gloriously.

She remembered exactly where she had been sitting when she'd read the telegram in 1944, which officially brought her the news that her eldest son had been killed in action in the South Pacific. She grieved again for the loss of her canine companions, Licorice and Vanilla, who had walked so many miles with her on the beach and had snuggled next to her on the cold winter nights. She grieved that an era was gone forever, that such an important part of her life had come to an end.

Rose Cottage would always be a part of her, and Elizabeth had more happy memories than she had reasons to be sad. She remembered the long summer days spent in her garden and on her sailboat. She remembered the winter evenings she had spent listening to the news of the war on the radio and knitting bandages by the fire in her cozy living room. She remembered picking a ripe tomato from her garden, sprinkling it with salt and pepper, and eating it from her hand like an apple. She remembered the many magnificent sunsets of the summer and the wild gray days of winter. She had a thousand happy things to think about as she looked back on her life. She'd lived an adventure of her own design and found contentment. Her children and grandchildren were already planning a new, bigger summer beach house on the property. It was time to move on and embrace a new era.

The new beach house was built, and the family spent many happy summers enjoying the ocean. Elizabeth died in 1996, three weeks after she celebrated her one-hundredth birthday. She had never expected to live so long. One of her grandchildren, Lowell James, was a journalist and wanted to write a book about his grandmother. Elizabeth had kept a journal off and on during her life, and she had been particularly faithful about writing down her thoughts during the years of World War Two.

Elizabeth Darling James had been an excellent photographer. Almost all of her work was done in black and white, and she had taken hundreds of photos during the years she had lived at Rose Cottage. Lowell James had adored his grandmother, who had been a fascinating person. He thought the photos she had taken and the journals she had kept could become a wonderful memoir about her life during the war years.

When he sorted through her photos, Lowell found that most of the ones she'd taken before moving to Delaware had been developed in her own dark room at the house in Washington D.C. Elizabeth had dated those on the back in her own handwriting. Kodak had developed the pictures she'd taken during her years in Bethany Beach and stamped the date on the back of each print. Lowell sorted the photos by year and came across several that aroused his curiosity. Most of the photos from the early years in D.C. were of his father and his aunts and uncles at a variety of family events and celebrations, trips abroad, and other vacations. During the years she had lived in Delaware, his grandmother had begun to take some pictures in color. She had taken photos of her house and gardens at the beach. There were countless pictures of sunsets and sunrises, *rosa rugosa* and hydrangea bushes, and dogs.

Among the puzzling photos Lowell discovered in the collection were several close-ups of a man's face. They'd been developed in 1942. The man was not anybody Lowell recognized. He certainly was not a member of the family. He had a dark beard and was standing near the water's edge. His back was to the ocean, and he was facing Rose Cottage. What was unusual about these photos was that the man Elizabeth had photographed held a tiny Minox camera in front of his face in several of the shots. Lowell had not realized the famous German mini-camera had been available for sale to the public in 1942. It must have cost the man a fortune to buy one at the time.

Lowell's grandmother had taken pictures of a man taking pictures of her and her house. She had marked these few photos on the back with the note: photo shot April 10, 1942 7:30 a.m. For some reason, Elizabeth James had singled out these photos, not only with a date, but also with a specific time of day. Lowell set these photos of the stranger aside and made a note to check his grandmother's journal for that day, April 10, 1942.

When he looked at Elizabeth's journal, he read and reread the detailed account of her awakening in the middle of the night because the dogs were growling. Elizabeth had recounted in detail her discovery of the bearded man who was using the pump on her porch. Lowell smiled as he read his grandmother's story about how she had fired birdshot into the air to frighten the intruder and followed him down the beach in her dressing gown. Lowell was intrigued that the man had escaped by climbing into a waiting raft and rowing himself out into the ocean. Who would do something like that unless they had a ship — or a U-boat — waiting for them somewhere out there? The bearded fellow couldn't have expected to row very far or for very long in a flimsy raft headed for France.

The same man with a beard reappeared two days later on the beach in front of Rose Cottage with his Minox camera. According to her journal, Elizabeth was quite certain he was the same person who had been drinking water from her pump a few nights earlier. She had taken several photos of the mystery man and was intrigued and concerned about why he was taking pictures of her house.

Elizabeth had recorded her discovery of the shovel, the trolley, and the rope, all of which she had turned over to the authorities in Georgetown. Elizabeth documented everything. She'd left in her journal the photos she had taken of these artifacts before she relinquished them to the Sussex County sheriff. She remarked in her journal that the sheriff, who had pretty much looked blank when she had earlier reported seeing ships burning off the coast in front of Rose Cottage, seemed more interested in examining the hard evidence her latest find had produced. Eye witness anecdotes and accounts of burning ships from older women didn't hold as much sway as real wood, metal, and hemp objects.

Lowell James had been born in December of 1944. He'd never known his biological father. His mother had been within days of giving birth to Lowell when she learned that her husband was missing and believed killed in action in the South Pacific. His ship had been hit by a Kamikaze pilot in the Gulf of Leyte, and his body was never recovered from the sea. Lowell's mother remarried a few years after the end of the war, and Lowell grew up with a wonderful and loving stepfather. His stepfather had adopted him and adored him beyond reason. No one could have wished for a more wonderful father figure in one's life. Lowell's interest in researching and writing about World War Two was a natural outgrowth of his lifetime curiosity about that time in history. Many "war babies" shared this fascination with the events of those years during which the United States and its allies fought the forces of evil in the world. These were the triumphs and the tragedies, which shaped their earliest years.

As time passed, Lowell's family had sold off most of the acres that had been a part of the original Rose Cottage property. A large development of beach houses had grown up beside the house the family had built after the 1962 northeastern storm. The small piece of property that was left surrounding the house was very valuable. All ocean front property demanded a premium price. In 2007 the forty-five-year-old house needed a new roof and new plumbing. Lowell's cousins, with whom he shared ownership of the family's 1960's beach house, were not as enamored with the place as he was. His relatives were living all over the United States and all over the world. Only a few had been helping to pay the property taxes and contributing toward maintaining the beach house's structural integrity. Lowell couldn't afford to buy out his relatives. Some of them needed money to put their kids through college. Most of them never used the beach house any more. One of his cousins lived in Hong Kong. Another cousin lived in Italy. One of his cousins loved the beach like Lowell did, but she and her family had bought their own place in Rehoboth.

With great sadness, Lowell agreed to sell the house and divide the proceeds from the sale among the heirs. Lowell couldn't afford to buy another place. It was the end of another era. The property was sold, and Lowell's family's ties to the property where Rose Cottage had once stood came to an end in 2008. The beach house was torn down and replaced with a development of very expensive new homes.

Chapter Thirteen

I Have a Photograph

Last Summer

The force was with them! Or at least the law in the state of Delaware was with them. Both Abbey and Gretchen had been able to determine that, in the state of Delaware, the finder's keeper's law was in effect. Originating from the French word "trouver" which means "to find," the law was called "treasure trove," meaning found treasure. The treasure the girls had found on the beach belonged to them. It did not belong to whoever owned the beach, and it did not belong to the State of Delaware. This news that the treasure was legally theirs was very exciting for everybody.

Gram found the old German-English dictionary from her graduate school days. Years ago, she had taken a summer class to learn to read German so she could pass a reading exam for a graduate degree. It had been a very long time since she had used the dictionary or tried to read anything in German. Grandpa Bob had studied German in high school, but that too had been a very long time ago. Gram and Bob thought they were going to need their knowledge of German to be able to read the papers that Lane and Louisa had found at the bottom of their trunk. Because the lettering on the inside of the top of the trunk had been in pre-World War Two German script, everyone assumed the papers inside the trunk would be in German.

Gram and Bob poured over the papers that Lane and Louisa had found. Whoever put the papers in the trunk had not intended for it to be buried in the sand for decades, and the papers inside had suffered from the years that had passed. Some of the papers were just too old and crumbly to read. Imagine their shock when Gram and Bob realized that the only papers and documents that were still legible were all in English! How could that be? But it was true, and they could easily read everything that was salvageable from inside the trunk.

One of the few things in the trunk, which had withstood the ravages of time, was a United States passport. It had been issued in Washington D.C. in 1938 to a man named Alexander Foster Callahan, which did not sound like the name of a German person. The passport showed a picture of a handsome young man with dark hair and dark eyes and said that the holder of the passport had been born in Erie, Pennsylvania on October 9, 1915. Among the other documents from the trunk that remained intact was a birth certificate from Erie County in Pennsylvania for this same man. The birth certificate confirmed Callahan's date of birth.

Other papers that remained intact included maps and plats of property in the area of Roxana, Delaware. The yellowed and torn newspaper articles were disintegrating. These clippings, from newspapers dated 1942, looked like advertisements for farms that had been for sale in Sussex County. Some papers in the collection appeared to be official military papers from the United States Navy, but the ink had faded so badly on these documents, they were impossible to read. Gram was sorry that the military paperwork couldn't be deciphered. Being able to read it might have shed some light on who Alexander Foster Callahan had been. As soon as Gram touched most of the paper, especially the newspaper, it fell apart in her hands. Only the passport and the birth certificate could be saved.

Gram wondered if the trunk had once belonged to Alexander Foster Callahan. If so, why had he chosen to bury so much gold and other valuables, as well as his passport, in the sand? This was the question everybody wanted answered. Furthermore, if Alexander had buried the trunk, why had he never returned to dig it up? Why would anyone leave a trunk full of so much treasure abandoned at the beach for all those years? The lettering on the inside of the trunk itself was in German, but the passport and the paperwork for Mr. Callahan were in English. Had the owner of the trunk been a German, or had he been an American? It was a mystery.

If he were still alive, Alexander Foster Callahan would have been more than one hundred years old this year. Chances were that he was deceased, since not many people live to be that old. Gram decided she had to try to find out more about Callahan. She searched the Internet, then made some phone calls to Erie County in Pennsylvania. She didn't want to go to the courthouse in Erie County to make inquiries in person, so she hired a private investigator to do the legwork for her. She wanted to know if Callahan's birth certificate and passport were genuine. She wanted to try to find out what had happened to him. When had he died? Did he have any children or other heirs? Gram wanted to know everything there was to know about Alexander Foster Callahan. If he or his potential heirs could be located, they might have a legal or a moral claim to the treasure. It was important that all avenues to find Callahan be explored.

Within a week, Gram heard back from the private investigator. The PI had located a birth certificate for a man with that exact name and birthday in the Erie County, Pennsylvania courthouse. A person named Alexander Foster Callahan had indeed been born on October 9, 1915 in Erie, Pennsylvania. The equally interesting and somewhat surprising thing was that the PI, in addition to finding the man's birth certificate, had also found his death certificate. The death certificate for Alexander Foster Callahan was dated February 3, 1916. The infant had died of pneumonia when he was almost four months old. The investigator had gone a step further and checked old newspaper obituaries from that period. Somebody had gone to the trouble of transferring decades of old local newspapers onto microfiche, so these historic records were now available to the public. The PI had found a short obituary in the newspaper, which confirmed that Alexander Foster Callahan had died as an infant in the winter of 1916.

Intrigued by the apparent death of this man when he was a baby, Gram's investigator asked her permission to follow up on Callahan's passport. The passport stated that it had been issued in Washington, D.C. in 1938 when Alexander Foster Callahan would have been twenty-three years old. The PI pulled some strings and found someone who could access old records at the Department of State. As a result of his inquiries, he discovered that no United States passport had ever been issued to anybody named Alexander Foster Callahan in 1938. The number on the passport was not a number the State Department had ever used. The passport was a fake, a phony, a forgery.

The quality of the forged passport had all the earmarks of a very professional job of counterfeiting. Whoever had fabricated the passport had started with a real blank U.S. passport. The forger had found the name of a real United

States citizen who had a real birth certificate. This real person had died in infancy. The professional forger had used authentic birth certificate information to make a phony passport in the name of Alexander Foster Callahan. It was expertly done. Whoever the person using Alexander Foster Callahan's identity had been, he had paid a great deal of money for such a convincing fake. The real Callahan would never come forward to apply for a passport of his own. If no one had investigated, the ruse would never have been exposed.

Whoever had buried all that gold and currency and all those diamonds, it had not been Alexander Foster Callahan from Erie, Pennsylvania. After all the possible avenues of investigation had been exhausted, Gram felt as if she had done everything she could to try to locate the owner of the trunk. With no real clues about the German person he might have once been, it seemed that the real identity of the person who had buried the treasure in the sand would forever remain a mystery.

– Chapter Fourteen –

I Have a Photograph, Too

Last Summer

After Lowell James retired from his job as a television anchorman and journalist, he decided to follow his passion and become a full-time writer. He worked on his grandmother's memoirs for more than two years. He found a publisher, and his book was a success. His audience was World War Two buffs and others interested in history and military strategy. After his book was published, he had a book signing in Bethany Beach. *A View From the Dunes: World War Two Life on the Delaware Homefront* was a tribute to his grandmother's love of the place, and it caught on with people intrigued by Lowell's accounts of the U-boat attacks along the Atlantic coast in the early days of the United States' entry into World War Two. Lowell made a nice income from the book, but the most important result of his publication was the recognition and celebrity he earned. His book was well written and interesting to a wide variety of readers.

Lowell had included many of his grandmother's photographs in the book, which had added to the narrative's appeal. One of the photos was of the mystery man holding the Minox, and Lowell labeled it "Mystery Man on the Beach." He also included his grandmother's journal entries that referred to the man and the exact date and time she had taken the pictures with her own camera. One of the people who bought a copy of Lowell's book at the Bethany Beach signing was another World War Two history enthusiast who lived in Lewes, Delaware. Crawford Jackson was a retired United States Army Colonel. He volunteered at the Fort Miles Historical Area at Cape Henlopen State Park and gave tours there. He could hardly wait to begin reading the book written about the war years on the beach so close to his own home. He had often wondered what it had been like to live at the beach during World War Two. He had his new book signed by the author and took it with him to the Parkway Restaurant in Bethany Beach where he was meeting a friend for dinner. The retired Colonel arrived a little early and asked to be seated while he waited for his friend.

He was thumbing through his copy of *A View From the Dunes: World War Two Life on the Delaware Homefront* when he came across the photograph "Mystery Man on the Beach." The black and white photo had faded somewhat over the years, but it had been taken with an old-fashioned telephoto lens and was an excellent close-up of the man's face. Something about that face caught the Colonel's eye, and he realized that somewhere, he had seen another photograph of this same man. He wracked his brain to remember where he had seen it. Jackson's friend arrived for dinner, and somewhere between the homemade gazpacho with jumbo lump crabmeat and the excellent "steak and cake" with mashed potatoes and roasted asparagus, Colonel Jackson remembered where he had seen another photo of the man with the beard.

The Colonel had seen this man's face in a photograph at Cape Henlopen State Park in one of the exhibits in the Fort Miles Historical Area. Jackson gave tours of the bunkers and other facilities at Fort Miles. He was available at the park for special events and had been one of the founders of the Fort Miles Historical Association, which worked in partnership with Delaware State Parks. The exhibit that Jackson recalled had been compiled by historians at Fort Miles when they were researching Operation Drumbeat.

The early years of 1942, when Germany's U-boats had inflicted terrible carnage on the United States' Merchant Marine fleet, was a period that interested all naval historians. Archivists in Germany had sent several interesting photos and documents, which told the story of those deadly months from the point of view of the German U-boat crews and commanders. One of the photographs the Germans had sent to Fort Miles was a formal photograph of the entire crew of one of the U-boats that had frequented the Delaware coast during what the Germans had called "The Second Happy Time." The U-boat in question had spent time prowling the waters around the mouth of the Delaware Bay and had torpedoed ships off the coast of Delaware. In December of 1941, someone had taken a posed photograph of the U-boat crew before it left its berth in France to sail across the Atlantic Ocean to undertake its deadly activities preying on U.S. ships. The men were arranged in two rows, one sitting and one standing behind. That U-boat and its ill-fated crew had finally met their own demise when they had been attacked by a United States Coast Guard vessel off the coast of New Jersey in the late summer of 1942. All hands went down with the U-boat near Barnegat Light as the submarine was beginning its return voyage to German-occupied France. The Colonel was certain the man in both photographs was the same person, but he would take his copy of *A View From the Dunes* to the museum and compare the photographs side by side.

If the same man were in both photos, it would mean that a member of a German U-boat crew had actually come ashore one morning and taken pictures of Elizabeth and Rose Cottage. "Mystery Man" would be a mystery no more. He might even be able to be identified by a name. It would be shocking to the American public that the Germans had been able to come and go ashore at will. These enemy combatants had been free to walk on the beaches of the precious American homeland, take pictures, and safely return to their U-boats. They had been able to enter the United States, make themselves at home, and leave again, mostly without anybody noticing they had paid a visit.

The next day Colonel Jackson compared the photos. Sure enough, his photographic memory had not failed him. There was Reinhard Hoffman and the rest of his U-boat crew lined up for a formal photographic portrait taken before leaving on a submarine voyage. Jackson was excited that he had been able to identify "Mystery Man on the Beach," the picture in Lowell James' book. Not only did he confirm that the man who had been standing on the sand in April of 1942 taking pictures of James's grandmother had been a member of a German U-boat crew, the Colonel was able to give "Mystery Man" a name.

He was anxious to get in touch with Lowell James and tell him what he had discovered. A piece of the mystery was solved. What remained unknown was why Reinhard Hoffman would have been standing on the sand in Bethany Beach on the morning of April 10, 1942 taking pictures of Elizabeth Darling James and Rose Cottage. Why did the man want a photo of Elizabeth's house? That might remain a mystery for the ages.

– Chapter Fifteen –

Pieces of the Puzzle

Last Year

The Wall Street Journal had given the book good reviews, and Grandpa Bob was a history buff. He mostly read books about the Revolutionary War, but this story interested him because he was a "war baby" born in 1943 and because he owned a house near the town of Bethany Beach. He'd read the review of *A View from the Dunes: World War Two Life on the Delaware Homefront* and was anxious to get a copy. Written by the woman's grandson, Lowell James, who was now in his early seventies, it was the story of Elizabeth Darling James, a woman who had lived in a beach cottage north of Bethany Beach, and the journal she had kept during World War Two.

He'd enjoyed reading the book and thought Gram would really like it, too. Gram read all the time and always had three or four books going at once. She preferred to read on her Kindle because she could read late into the night and early in the morning without turning on any lights. The Kindle was backlit and easy to read in the dark. She finally got around to reading the book Grandpa Bob had recommended to her and found it to be an enchanting narrative about a very interesting woman. Gram was captivated by the many old photographs that were included in the book, and she, too, loved the story because it took place near Bethany Beach where she and Grandpa Bob had their beach house.

The first time Gram looked through the photos, she paused when she saw "Mystery Man on the Beach." Gram always loved a mystery, and there was something about this one that intrigued her. She kept coming back to the page that showed the photo of the man holding a tiny Minox camera. He had a mustache and a long dark beard, so his face was mostly obscured by facial hair. But the man's dark, piercing eyes and the thick, bushy eyebrows caught Gram's attention and tugged at her memory. She reread the book a couple of times hoping she could put her finger on what was bothering her.

One night, Gram's Kindle was lying on the bed, and it was opened to the photograph of "Mystery Man on the Beach" in *A View from the Dunes*. A magazine lay across the bottom half of the face on the screen of the Kindle, and only the upper half of the man's face was visible. Gram looked down for the umpteenth time at the deeply set dark eyes and bushy eyebrows. It hit her all of a sudden. Those eyes looked like they belonged to the man in the Alexander Foster Callahan passport picture. "Mystery Man on the Beach" in Lowell James' book was the same person as Gram's mystery man from the 1938 passport photo. The man pictured in the passport was clean-shaven, and in the photo from the book taken on the beach in 1942, the man's mustache and long, dark beard were distracting. But if one looked at just the eyes and blocked the superfluous facial hair from the picture, anyone could see that the eyes and the eyebrows were exactly the same. There was no doubt about it. The two mystery men were one.

Gram could not wait to contact Lowell James with her information, but that would be easier said than done. Apparently, when one publishes a book that has a mysterious photo in it, the author receives countless communications from people in the public who think they can identify that person and solve the mystery. This was the case with Lowell James. He'd heard from hundreds of readers who were sure they knew "Mystery Man on the Beach." At first Lowell had tried to follow up on each lead and had responded politely to those who were certain it was their Uncle Manfred who had gone missing in 1935 or their cousin who had never returned from the Allied Front in France. He'd finally had to give up responding to those who contacted him about the mystery man.

Colonel Crawford Jackson had trouble getting Lowell James's attention about his discovery in the exhibit at Cape Henlopen State Park. Jackson sent Lowell James copies that showed Reinhard Hoffman's photograph with his U-boat crew. James finally responded to Jackson's communications and expressed delight that he finally had a name for "Mystery Man on the Beach." That part of the mystery was solved. Lowell now knew the name of the bearded man in the photograph but still didn't know why Reinhard Hoffman happened to be on the beach in Delaware in April of 1942.

Lowell James officially closed the chapter on the identity of "Mystery Man on the Beach" and ignored all future letters and emails from those who thought they knew the man. Lowell had a reporter from the *Coastal Point*, a Sussex County local weekly newspaper, do a follow-up story to his book. The article was about how "Mystery Man on the Beach" was a mystery no more. He had a name, and his picture could be seen by one and all at Fort Miles. Both photographs were included as part of the Coastal Point article, and it was obvious that these two men with long, dark beards were the same person. Mystery solved!

Gram wrote a letter to Lowell James and included copies of the picture from the book and the picture from the passport. Gram told James in her letter the story of how she had happened to have in her possession the fake passport with Alexander Foster Callahan's name on it. She told him about the investigation she had pursued into Callahan's background and what the results of that investigation had been. She was certain the man in Lowell's photo was the same man whose phony passport had been found in the trunk buried in the sand.

Lowell James eventually did read the letter Gram had written him. He wrote back and told her he agreed with her that the two photographs were of the same person. He was happy to tell her that he had been able to identify the man and that his real name, indeed his German name, was Reinhard Hoffman. Lowell told her he had learned the German U-boat crew member's identity through another person who had read the book about his grandmother. He told her she could see the man's photo in an exhibit at Cape Henlopen State Park.

Gram was thrilled to learn the real name of the man whose forged passport photo had haunted her. She learned from Lowell James that Reinhard Hoffman had died in the late summer of 1942. She wondered if she should try to find Hoffman's family and looked into tracking Hoffman's personal history in pre-war Europe. Because so many years had passed and because there had been so much destruction of documents and physical property in Germany as a result of the war, she decided it was a dead end. She briefly felt guilty about the decision to drop her inquiries. She could speculate about why Hoffman had paid a great sum of money to buy a forged United States passport. She could speculate about why Hoffman may or may not have been the person who had buried the trunk full of treasure in the sand. In the end, she concluded that the Nazis had aggressively and enthusiastically brought their reign of death and destruction to the shores of Delaware in the early days of 1942 with Operation Drumbeat. They had ultimately lost the war. Whoever had left treasure buried in the sand on the beach had abandoned it. It was treasure lost and treasure found. In 1828 when the Jacksonian Democrats had won the presidential election, New York Senator William L. Marcy said, "To the victor belong the spoils." Gram decided she would accept without guilt what time and tides had brought to her family in Bethany Beach.

– Chapter Sixteen –

Back to the Future

Last Year

Northeastern storms and hurricanes periodically destroy the beach and the dunes along the Atlantic coast. Sand is carried out to sea, then washed back in and redeposited. The forces of nature devastate and rebuild over the centuries as tidal surges, winds, and coastal flooding reshape the shoreline. Houses, vegetation, boats, and people are lost in the ocean's fury. Did either of Reinhard's buried treasures survive this ebb and flow? Was either trunk captured by the ocean's tumult? Was either one returned to the sand? Did one or both remain snuggly hidden in their original hiding places in the dunes? No one would ever know exactly what journey these two chests of riches had made in the years after 1942. Almost seventy-five years later, one long-hidden trunk was recovered serendipitously in the sand on a summer morning by two young girls who were "digging to China."

The week of July Fourth had been unlike any other beach vacation Lane and Louisa's family had experienced. As soon as the banks opened, the adults had carried plastic containers full of gold, coins, and money and secured them in safety deposit boxes. Choosing not to put all their treasure in one bank complicated the process; there were signature cards, keys, and other details to take care of. The adults spent a great deal of time on their cell phones talking to lawyers, numismatists, an undersecretary of the United States Treasury, officials who worked for the State of Delaware, several accountants, and other specialists in a variety of fields.

One lawyer, whose expertise seemed to carry the most weight, was a woman who advised those who had won big money in the Powerball, Mega Millions, and other lottery jackpots. She knew how to structure the financial windfall of lottery winners, so they were able to keep the government from confiscating so much of their winnings in taxes.

The bottom line was that in Delaware, "Treasure Trove" belonged to the finder. Without dispute, the treasure belonged to the lucky kids who had been digging in the sand. That was the good news. The bad news was that it would be taxed as income. As unfair as that might seem, it was just like winning the lottery. Hence, the importance of the lawyer who knew how to allocate and protect the windfall.

A generous educational trust would be set up for the five grandchildren. Lane and Louisa had recovered the treasure, but they were minors, which added another level of legal complication to the situation. The adults wanted to respect the fact that the two girls had been the ones to find and save the treasure. Without their quick thinking in securing the contents of the trunk, there would be nothing to discuss. The family held a special meeting to determine what would be done with the remainder of their wealth.

The proposal that seemed to be the most popular with the children was to establish a beach stabilization program for the communities along the Delaware coast. In January, northeastern storm Jason had hovered over the Delaware beaches for days and given them a serious beating. The dune had been completely destroyed, and the dune fences had been carried away in the storm surge. Jonas had so badly eroded the beach at Sandpiper Dunes and all the other developments along the coast that it had been necessary for the Delaware Department of Natural Resources to bulldoze sand out of the ocean to restore the dunes on all the beaches north and south of Bethany Beach. The dune had been rebuilt, but the dune grass that held the sand in place was gone. New dune grass would be planted in the fall. Louisa and Lane and their brothers had been told repeatedly how lucky they were to have had any beach at all to play on that summer.

No hurricane or Northeastern storm in decades had done as much damage as Jonas. Lane and Louisa believed that Jonas might have brought the treasure to them. The beach restoration fund would pay to plant dune grass, replace dune fences, and undertake other worthy beach preservation and restoration projects to save the beaches for future generations.

Austin and Aunt Joanie from California wanted another mission for the family's foundation. They wanted some of the treasure to be used to buy undeveloped properties that came on the market to prevent the land from being used for more houses. They wanted a legacy that would protect the beach and nearby wetlands from overdevelopment. It was an East Coast versus West Coast discussion and represented a kind of compromise.

Abbey was going to administer the Burkhart Family Educational Trust. Gretchen and Joanie would administer the Burkhart Beach Protection and Restoration Initiative and the Burkhart Beach and Wetlands Preservation Foundation. Gretchen and the children would decide which beach protection and restoration projects would be funded, and Joanie and Austin would oversee the purchase of undeveloped property.

The five cousins were happy with the decisions that had been made. They were the heirs, not only to their family's financial assets, but also to the beach that would be saved and the land that would be left undeveloped. The children deserved a say in how their secret in the sand would be spent to restore and to preserve their beach for the future. After all, the future was theirs.